Unexpected World

The EMP Survivor Series – Book 1
by Chris Pike

Unexpected World
by Chris Pike
Copyright © 2016. All Rights Reserved
Formatted for print by MPP Freelance

This book is a work of fiction. People, places, events, and situations are the product of the author's imagination. Any resemblance to actual persons, living or dead, or historical events, is purely coincidental.

Prologue

The fight of his life was about to begin.

A strong man with a purpose emerged from the tangled, swampy woods of the Louisiana back county. His shirt and jeans, seasoned by the journey, were stiff and worn. A big dog walked in step by his side, waiting for instruction. The man scanned the clearing, looking for movement on the lake.

Unknown to the man, a monster alligator had floated silently for hours, sometimes completely submerged, hidden in the murky swamp, waiting, watching, biding its time.

Prey would come.

It always did.

Dark eyes bobbed on the surface. Shore birds pecked the shallow water for minnows or bugs, their movements jerky and wary.

A salty breeze carried a scent, and the dog lifted its

snout, tasting the air, searching for the meaning of the unusual scent. The dog, sensing the unseen danger, stayed close to the man, nudging him away from the danger. The man did not heed the dog's warning, and instead offered a warm hand to the dog to comfort him.

A flap of wings.

Whoosh.

The dog flinched.

The birds scattered to the treetops.

The man said something to his faithful dog. Maybe *sit* or *stay.* Something the dog understood.

He waded into the knee-deep swamp water to check the fish trap he had set earlier in the day.

A thousand pounds of prehistoric instinct swiveled cold black eyes in the direction of the movement, zeroing in on its prey with deadly precision. The massive beast slithered through the water, a quiet ripple the only evidence death was moments away.

Black, reptilian eyes focused like lasers on its prey.

A crow cawed, then another, a foreboding chorus echoing in the wilderness.

The man looked skyward, squinting through the treetops as he looped the nylon cord hand over hand. Droplets of water dripped from the cord.

The alligator submerged.

The dog rose, whining.

"Stay," the man said, motioning with his hand. The dutiful dog did as told and lowered himself into the soft earth next to a log. His muscles twitched in nervous anticipation, his eyes bouncing from the man to the water and beyond.

Oblivious to the danger, the man returned to his chore of checking the fish trap made from bark strips and grapevine woven together into a cone. He pulled on the nylon cord like a fisherman would trawl a line, until the top of the trap breached the surface.

The trapped fish wiggled and splashed, darting, trying to escape, instinct alerting them to the massive predator lurking in the shallows.

The dog whined.

The alligator got closer.

The man, puzzled at the strange behavior of the fish, had a fleeting memory of seeing a school of fish behave in the same manner of an approaching killer whale. It was something he had seen on the Nat Geo channel one lazy afternoon as he whiled the time away. Standing in the water, his mind searched for the underlying meaning and a brief flicker of understanding came to him. In that millisecond when his mind finally understood until his body could react, the expression of his face captured the realization of horror. He went to turn and—

Water exploded like an erupting volcano!

He caught a brief glimpse of the beast and fully understood the deadliness of the situation.

The nylon cord fell limp into the water.

He turned to flee but before he could, the thousand pound reptile twisted its body, and with pure brute power slammed the man down, knocking him into the water. His face mashed into the muck and he tasted the stink of the mud.

The trapped fish scattered from the crumpled trap.

Three thousand pounds of biting pressure clamped down on the man's leg, forcing him further underwater. The alligator had the man in a death roll, thrashing and spinning to disorient him in the dark water. The strategy to drown its prey had worked well through the millennia for the apex predator.

The man struggled desperately to keep from inhaling the cold swamp water. His heart hammered against his chest like it was about to explode while his lungs screamed for air.

The dog bolted to the water's edge, barking and

snapping, running along the shore. Instinct told him to be wary.

In his adrenaline-charged state, the man didn't feel the crushing weight against his leg or the chilling effects of the water soaking his soul.

He had a quick thought about how much longer he could hold his breath before he blacked out. *Maybe a few seconds,* he thought.

He clawed the water searching for anything to hold onto, a tree limb, a submerged stump, but all he felt was the rough, cold, leathery skin of the alligator.

His eyes were shut tight, his lips pressed hard together. His heart pounded. He needed to breathe...

Disoriented, he didn't know which way was up to the surface to the air he needed.

In a desperate effort, he thrust his arm into the alligator's mouth, between the bone-crushing teeth, the massive jaw. He stretched further, reaching for the soft palate, to rip it out. Further his hand explored, touching the bony ridges of the mouth.

The sensation of his life ebbing away came to him and his thoughts became fuzzy. Though his eyes were closed, stars appeared against the backdrop of his life. A shimmering bright light flooded his vision, dimming his awareness of the continued thrashing.

Mud and debris swirled around them.

His arm felt weak.

He felt his life slipping away...

The overpowering need to breathe vanished, and he no longer searched for the beast's throat in a last attempt to free himself. With his strength waning, his body rolled soundlessly in the dark water.

His mind transported him to images of his wife, when they were young, when the world was different, when the world was safe...before she had died.

They were in bed, their bodies naked under the cool

cotton sheets. His wife's hair cascaded over him and he took a handful, taking in a breath of her essence. She playfully ran a finger over his chest, tickling him.

Dying wasn't so bad after all.

Still, he was somewhat aware of the power pummeling his body, of being dragged deeper through the water.

He opened his eyes to a facet of consciousness refusing to surrender to death, a spark of life flickering in the dank, dirty swamp. His dying body violently convulsed in an automatic survival response, struggling to live.

The images came again and he had a vague sensation of walking, his wife beside him. She was smiling and laughing. He hadn't seen her in so long, and he ached to be reunited with her, even if it had to be in death. She was so young and pretty. Her sun-kissed hair flowed across her shoulders.

She held out a hand, motioning for him to take it, whispering words he couldn't understand.

He reached for her hand, eager to thread his fingers through hers.

To touch her once more.

She was just out of reach. Inches away.

Her smile faded and an indescribable sadness stretched across her beautiful features. She turned her back on him, walking away.

"Come back," he pleaded. She demurely cast a glance over her shoulder at him, her eyes downcast...

He ran to her. "Don't go," he said. "I want to stay with you and—"

Boom!

Silence.

Boom!

The violent sounds jolted him back to reality and to the pain of dying.

He'd never imagined dying like this. After everything he had been through, after fighting to live for so long, this was it, and nobody would know what happened to him. Worst of all, he would never fulfill the promise he had made.

He shuddered once, his body fell limp, and he submitted to the blackness closing around him.

Chapter 1

A verdict was expected any minute and the tension in the courtroom was palpable.

Deputy District Attorney Dillon Stockdale sat in his assigned seat on the top floor of the venerable Harris County Courthouse in Houston, Texas.

He was itching to get the show on the road and then blow out of town. He needed a little R&R after the intense five week trial of testimony, objections, highly paid experts, and an endless amount of legal drivel. He was considering a change of profession. What he didn't know was that he'd get his wish sooner than expected.

It had been a hard fight between Dillon and defense attorney Holly Hudson.

Dillon glowered at the smug defendant, Cole Cassel, sitting at the next table. A three piece suit couldn't make even the sorriest mutt look like a show dog, and the suit Cole had on looked like it had come from a high-end tailor. Dillon's affordable suit, on the other hand, had been bought off the rack at a men's chain store.

If Cole thought he could waltz into Houston from New Orleans and establish a new territory by offing a competitor, he hadn't planned on the district attorney's tenacity and bullheaded attitude.

Cole was a bigwig in the Big Easy, and coming to H-town he thought he could throw around some of that Cajun attitude. He hadn't counted on crossing paths with Dillon Stockdale.

How the defendant was able to afford Holly Hudson was anybody's guess. Drug money must have been funneled her way, which gave Dillon more fodder for not liking her. He couldn't wrap his mind around why she had taken this sorry excuse for a human as a client. Normally her clients were the fat cats of the corporate world, those that schemed as they sat at a mahogany table in a corner office devising ways to cheat the hardworking, good people of America out of their money.

The jurors had been out for two days when the judge reconvened the court. A verdict had finally been decided.

Dillon palmed his head and let his hand stay there. He nervously tapped a pencil on the desk, waiting for the verdict.

Any minute now the jurors should file into the courtroom and take their seats.

He glanced at Cole, who returned a snide smile then mouthed the words *not guilty*. Holly pretended to be busy reviewing the case as she shuffled papers in her briefcase.

This hadn't been the first time Dillon had tangled with Holly Hudson. He had to admit, she was a first rate attorney with a pedigree to match. Magna Cum Laude, Harvard Law School. Dillon had to scratch and claw his way through a local law school, fighting for passing grades. His pedigree came from the county dog pound.

Talk was Holly had inherited a prime spread of ranchland in East Texas soaked in rich black oil, so it was hard for Dillon to understand why she was defending the scum of the Earth.

If Dillon had a spread like that, he'd ditch his suit for a pair of Wranglers, a good horse, and a Ford truck. City living was getting weary.

The jurors filed into the courtroom and took their seats.

Cole Cassel narrowed his eyes and glared at the jurors, studying them while they were seated. There were no smiles or relaxed postures, and the lady Cole had thrown flirty looks toward during the trial wouldn't make eye contact with him.

Rage built up in Cole, the rage of knowing he was powerless to prevent the inevitable. His breathing came fast and shallow. His chest rose and fell with each breath, and the vein on the side of his neck looked like it might pop. He balled his fists in anger. And it was all because of that bastard Stockdale.

"Has the jury reached a unanimous verdict?" the presiding judge asked the jury foreman.

"Yes, Your Honor, we have."

"Please hand the verdict form to the clerk."

The foreman extended his arm to the clerk, who then handed the slip of paper to the judge.

All eyes, including Dillon's, were on the judge. Dillon tried to discern any type of facial expression to indicate the verdict. No luck. The judge was a statue. Not even so much as a blink of an eye, a long exhale, or mouth twitch as he silently read the verdict.

As was customary, the judge handed the piece of paper back to the foreman for reading.

"Mr. Cassel, Counselor," the judge said, his eyes peeking over his reading glasses. "Please rise."

Cole did nothing.

"Mr. Cassel! Please rise."

Holly ordered, "Do as the judge says."

"No!" Cole yelled. He rocketed up and thumped his fists on the table. "I'm not standing for this! I ain't letting nobody pass judgement on me!" Directing his anger at Holly, he said in a low voice, "You bitch. I paid you for nuthin'. I told you what would happen if you lost. Remember?"

Holly shot her client an indignant expression. Through clenched teeth, she said, "Be quiet. I know what you told me."

A supporter of Cole's smiled a toothy grin and shouted from the back, fists pumping the air. "He ain't killed nobody! This trial has been rigged from the get go!" A chorus of hoots and howls erupted from the seating gallery.

"Order! There will be order in this court!" The judge pounded the gavel on the heavy desk. In a loud and commanding voice, he said, "Sit down, Mr. Cassel. You will conduct yourself appropriately while you're in my court."

The bailiff, Marcus Williams, a big guy that commanded respect, took a step forward with the intention to intimidate the defendant into sitting down.

Cole's glare wavered from the judge to the bailiff then back to Holly.

"Do as he says," Holly whispered, her jaw tight.

Cole snuck a peek at the bailiff. All 250 pounds of muscle glared straight at him. That and the fact his hand was on a mean-looking baton convinced Cole to sit down. Genetics had blessed Cole with height and strength. He had learned a long time ago how to bully his adversaries into submission. Holding a .38 Special while towering over someone went a long way to convince anyone. The bailiff wasn't intimidated one iota. He had about two inches and fifty pounds on Cole.

Cole sat down, begrudgingly.

Now he wasn't sure who to blame: his highly paid defense lawyer for being obviously incompetent or Mr. Hotshot district attorney for wanting another notch in his belt.

"I'll get you for this, Stockdale!" Cole shouted. "You'll see." Cole's temper got the best of him and without warning or indication, he shoved Holly Hudson aside and with the agility of a pole vaulter he lunged at Dillon.

Papers scattered and fell about the tables. A wooden chair clanged to the floor.

The judge sat stunned.

Sitting at the prosecutor's table, Dillon ducked his head just in time as Cole swung a wild fist that inadvertently collided with the jaw of a visitor sitting in the first row.

People scrambled to get out of the way.

Dillon acted quickly and shoved the chair back, stood up, and pivoted to face his opponent.

Cole swiveled around and like a bull gone mad, he lowered his head and charged Dillon, catching him at the waist.

Dillon grunted and leaned into Cole, pushing against him. He balled his fists and pummeled Cole, smashing him as a boxer would. A right hook, then a left one until the Cajun loosened his grip.

Dillon jerked a knee into Cole's stomach, lifting him up. The Cajun grunted a hard breath. Again Dillon kneed Cole, forcing him to let go. Cole stumbled back and doubled over in pain holding his stomach.

Bailiff Marcus Williams sprang into action and was on Cole like a hungry alley cat on a rat. Marcus wrapped his arms around the guy, holding him tight. "You need to calm down. You hear?" Marcus ordered. "I gotcha and I ain't lettin' go."

Cole struggled under the suffocating bear hug.

"They'll be order in this court! Order!" The judge pounded the gavel. "Mr. Cassel, I'll throw you in contempt of court if there's one more outburst from you. Understand?"

15

Holly said, "Yes, Your Honor, he understands."

"Nobody throws a temper tantrum in my court. You, Mr. Cassel," the judge said, wagging a finger, "will sit down and be quiet."

Cole Cassel's mouth was tight with anger, and sweat beaded his forehead. He threw a menacing look at the jurors who sat with their mouths agape. "Losers," he mumbled.

While the bailiff held Cole, Holly came up to him. Her voice was a whisper when she said, "Look at the judge and say yes."

"Yes." The word was barely audible.

"Louder," the judge ordered.

"Yes!" Cole yelled. "Good. Now since that's settled, there'll be a ten minute recess for everybody to collect themselves. After that we'll read the verdict."

Dillon Stockdale stood straight, pulled on both lapels of his suit, adjusted his tie, and cocked his neck to work out a kink that had been bothering him all day. He shot a cringe-worthy stare at Holly and her client then headed to the hallway to make a phone call.

Just another day at the office, Dillon mused.

Right. He'd win this case, he was sure of it. He could feel it in his bones that he was going to beat the revered Holly Hudson and put away Cole Cassel for a good, long time.

Dillon was bursting with excitement and had to share the news with somebody.

That *somebody* was his daughter, the only family member he had left.

Chapter 2

Cassie Stockdale and her best friend Vicky sat near the number one through thirty line at the Houston Hobby airport terminal, waiting for their numbers to be called for the short jaunt to New Orleans. They had signed in online at the earliest possible moment so they could get a good seat, and also to be the first to deplane.

She had a backpack looped over her shoulders containing the needed items like a large bottle of water, an energy bar, a flashlight, extra cash, a bag of pretzels, a chocolate bar with almonds, a laptop, and a change of clothes. The items she packed, sans the laptop, she had been drilled into her head by her safety conscious father, Dillon Stockdale.

Friends since they were in elementary school, Cassie and Vicky looked remarkably alike, with the same length and color of hair, same build, and they laughed about how they were dressed alike, wearing the same dark green Tulane t-shirt and jeans. People who didn't know them mistook them for sisters.

As Vicky rambled on about something, Cassie recalled her father's wise voice about the items she packed. He had been adamant regarding the reasons for carrying those items, for example in case there was a zombie outbreak or she was stranded in some godforsaken city without food, water, and clothes. Assuming the zombie outbreak was a humorous metaphor for an actual catastrophe such as a category 5 hurricane, Cassie heeded her father's advice.

Even though she wouldn't admit it to her father that she actually listened to him or fess up to packing the items he told her to, she was glad her father cared about her and had taught her to be self-sufficient.

"God helps those that help themselves," he would always say. It wasn't until she got older that she understood what that meant.

"Do you mind if I take the window seat?" Vicky asked. "You know how claustrophobic I get with so many people crammed into such a small space, not to mention the germs. I don't like strangers touching me either. Last time I was on a plane some huge fat guy sat next to me and his flab touched me." Vicky shuddered at the memory. "I forgot to ask, did you bring any hand sanitizer? I read an article about how germy planes are, especially the toilet and the—"

"Oh my God, will you stop!" Cassie said. "You can have the window seat. I don't care."

"Why so touchy?" Vicky asked, rolling her eyes. "Geez, it's not a long flight so I'll manage if you really have to have the window seat."

Cassie stared at Vicky.

"What?" Vicky said, eyes darting around.

"I already said you can have it. I really don't care."

"I'm sorry." Vicky put a hand on Cassie's arm. "I get nervous before flying."

"I know you do," Cassie said. "It's only a short flight from here to NOLA. And this is one of the safest airlines around. Besides, what could possibly happen on such a short flight?"

"Plenty of things, but I won't go there," Vicky said. "I'm sorry for being such a, you know... I'll buy you dinner when we get to NOLA. Gumbo at your favorite place?"

"Deal. I could use some good gumbo."

"Come on," Vicky said, "time for us to board."

Vicky pushed her way around a woman taking up the aisle and darted to the row she had her eyes on. While she struggled with the overhead bin, a man about the age of her dad asked, "Can I help you with that?"

"Sure," Vicky said.

"These things are tough sometimes," he said. "You remind me of my daughter."

"That's nice. Thank you," Vicky said.

The man said it was nothing and that he was glad to help, then squeezed his way down the aisle looking for a good seat.

"Come on, Cassie," Vicky said breathlessly, "let's sit in this row." Vicky quickly hopped over the first two seats and plopped down in the window seat. "Sit here before anyone else does." She motioned for Cassie to take the middle seat next to her.

The man who had helped Vicky with the overhead bin sat down two rows behind her. He mused how she reminded him of his daughter, and after his trip was over he planned to take his daughter out to dinner to celebrate her birthday. Buckling his seat belt, he looked up and noticed that Vicky had taken the window seat. Another passenger excused herself when she squeezed between him and the window seat. Distracted, he didn't see Cassie sit down next to Vicky.

After Cassie sat down, Vicky opened the window shade and checked the weather. It was a little overcast, a light breeze out of the south, which were excellent conditions for the pilots.

Cassie took off her backpack, retrieved a novel she had bought at the airport, and started flipping through it. With a shove of her foot she kicked the backpack under the seat in front of her.

Vicky kept an eye on the people entering the plane. There were the standard business types with suits and white shirts, a loosened tie, and lace-up black shoes. A mother holding a child walked down the aisle, another one hanging onto her pants followed behind clutching a toy. A team of what looked like soccer players arrived and promptly went to the back of a plane. More business travelers took seats until the plane was almost full.

"I guess you got lucky," Vicky said. "It looks like the flight attendant is getting ready to close the door."

Cassie breathed a sigh of relief. She didn't like sitting next to strangers either. Why the airplane had such small seats, she could never guess.

A flight attendant walked by, checking the overhead bins, securing them. She nodded at Cassie and said, "We'll be taking off soon."

"Thank goodness," Vicky said, leaning back in her chair. "I'm ready to get going."

Cassie opened the paperback and began reading. It was a break from the tedious material she had to read for the statistical class needed for one of her grad classes at Tulane. Soon she was immersed in the novel, completely forgetting about where she was and the noisy atmosphere of the cramped cabin. She was vaguely aware of someone standing next to her, asking her a question. She looked up.

"Is this seat taken?"

"Uh, no," Cassie said, eyeing the guy standing next to the empty seat. He had on loose-fitting jeans, hiking boots, and a t-shirt that appeared to have been worn more than once. She gave a shrug of her shoulders.

"Nobody is sitting there."

"Thanks," he said.

Cassie pretended to read the paperback but she couldn't help noticing how good looking the guy was. Tall, brown wavy hair, the t-shirt looked a little tight, but maybe that was from working out. He obviously worked out.

He sat down next to her and fiddled with the seat belt.

"I think you're sitting on it," he finally said.

"Sorry," Cassie said, lifting one side of her body. "There you go." She handed the seatbelt to him.

Vicky leaned into Cassie and whispered, "You have all the luck."

"What do you mean?"

"You know what I mean."

Cassie shifted uncomfortably in her seat. "You're the one that wanted the window seat, remember?"

"Yeah, yeah," Vicky said. Digging around in her purse, she pulled out earbuds, plugged them into her iPhone, tapped the phone a few times, then closed her eyes.

Good, Cassie thought. She'd finally have some peace and quiet and an easy 45 minute trip.

She couldn't even imagine how wrong she was.

Chapter 3

Finally the plane took off. Cassie dog-eared the paperback she was reading and placed it in her lap. She glanced out the window as the plane gathered altitude. Pockets of neighborhoods dotting the landscape raced by. A swimming pool here, one there. An undisturbed tract of pines among the four lane major streets, cars going in every direction.

Further the plane climbed and soon it was like the plane was floating on air. Sound became unnoticeable, time slowed. The higher the plane climbed, the smaller the land got, and the more peaceful it became.

For some reason she turned to face the aisle and when she did, she almost butted heads with the guy sitting next to her.

"Oh," Cassie said, putting a hand to her cheek. "I'm sorry, I didn't realize..."

"No problem," the guy sitting next to her said. "I'm the one who should be sorry. I didn't realize I was so close to you. I like to look out the window when the plane takes off because it grounds me. I like to know where I'm going."

"Me too," Cassie said. "I can't read until the plane has reached cruising altitude."

"What are you reading?"

"This?" Cassie said, somewhat embarrassed because it wasn't exactly thought provoking. "Something I picked up at the airport. It beats what I need to study when I get back to my apartment."

"You in school?" he asked.

"Yes. I'm getting a master's degree."

"At Tulane?"

"How did you know?"

"We *are* headed to New Orleans, and you do have on a Tulane shirt."

"Right," she said. "I forgot. And you? Where are you going?"

"Back to Tulane also."

"Small world," Cassie said.

"I just came back from a camping trip in Big Bend National Park. Sorry if I'm a little grungy," Ryan said.

"No problem."

"Me and a couple of buddies decided to get in a hike during the fall break before med school finals."

"You're in med school?"

"Yup."

"No kidding?"

"Nope."

Their conversation was interrupted by a flight attendant asking if they wanted something to drink, to which Cassie requested a Coke. "And you, sir?" the flight attendant asked.

"I'll have a Coke, too. Good for the digestion." He cracked a smile. There was a moment of silence until he said, "I'm Ryan Manning."

"Cassie Stockdale."

"Nice to meet you, Cassie," Ryan said. "Is that your nickname?"

"Yes."

"What's your real name?"

"I don't really like my real name."

"It'll be my secret," Ryan said.

Cassie waved him off. Vicky took her earbuds off, leaned in and said, "Calista. It means beautiful one."

Ryan said, "I like it." He thought about her name for a second and repeated it. "Calista. It *is* a beautiful name."

"Thank you," Cassie said, the heat in her cheeks rising. She elbowed Vicky and shot her a stare that meant business.

"What?" Vicky said. "Only trying to help." She rolled her eyes and put the earbuds back in her ears.

"Sorry," Cassie said. "She gets nervous flying."

"A lot people do," Ryan said.

"So," Cassie continued, "what kind of doctor do you want to be?"

"For right now I'm in internal medicine. This is my second year of med school so I still have time to decide. What are you studying?"

"Disaster Management."

Ryan nodded his approval. "After what happened to New Orleans after Katrina, I'm guessing you'll have no problem landing a job."

"That's what I'm hoping for. Besides, my dad always made sure we were prepared for the hurricane season, so it comes second nature to me. I'm from Houston and have lived through several hurricanes and tropical storms." Cassie nervously fanned the pages of the paperback she was holding trying to think of another question. "What made you want to become a doctor?"

"After I finished undergrad in biology I couldn't get a job, so I took a few courses to qualify as an EMT. I found out I liked helping people so decided to go whole hog and apply for med school."

Cassie laughed. "Whole hog! That's what my dad says."

"Sounds like my kind of guy," Ryan said. "Maybe someday I could meet him."

"Oh, yeah, sure," Cassie said, understanding the subtle connotation of that statement, which was fine by her because she'd immediately felt Ryan's presence the moment he sat down. Not something that was intimidating, rather a confidence he had in the way he talked, the way he carried himself. What little she knew about him she already liked. She guessed he was a little older than she was, perhaps by a couple of years. He had a casual way about him that made her feel at ease.

There was a lull in the conversation, the plane's engine droned on, and Cassie peered out the double-paned window.

The plane's flight path hugged the coast of Texas before crossing the Sabine River, which was the border between Texas and Louisiana. The Gulf of Mexico was to the right, and to the left, the Louisiana swamps and back country came into view.

"It looks so peaceful down there," Cassie said.

"Yeah, as long as you don't have to walk through it," Vicky said. She removed the earbuds, leaned into Cassie, and lowered her voice. "You have all the luck getting to sit next to a good-looking guy. If I had been sitting there some fat guy would have taken the seat."

"You were the one that wanted the window seat. Not me," Cassie reminded her again.

"Bad luck on my part," Vicky said. "I'm always getting the bad luck. Look out the window all you want. There are miles and miles of swamps and alligators. Stinky muck, full of leeches." She shivered. "There are things that can eat you in the swamp. I even read on the internet that someone spotted a black panther!"

"Oh, please," Cassie said. "You believe everything you

read?"

"Florida has cougars," Vicky harrumphed, "and the ones from Colorado and New Mexico have already moved south to Texas."

"Texas doesn't have cougars. That's ridiculous."

"They've been caught on game trail cameras."

"Maybe so. If I'm ever trapped in a swamp, or in the wilds of Texas, I'll be sure to keep a lookout for cougars," Cassie said.

"They're there. Mark my words," Vicky said. She opened the fashion magazine she had been holding and started flipping pages.

"Oh no," Cassie said. "I forgot to call my dad. I was supposed to have called him from the airport. I wonder if I could make a call this high up?"

"Try it," Ryan said. "I don't mean to eavesdrop, but couldn't help overhearing your conversation."

Cassie scratched the back of her head hoping that he hadn't heard all the conversation.

"Just don't let one of the flight attendants catch you because we're descending now," Ryan said.

Cassie tapped *Dad* in her contact list, brought the phone up to her ear, and waited for her dad to answer the phone.

A few rings later, she heard his familiar voice. "Hello?"

"Hey, Dad," Cassie said. "How's it going?"

"Hi, Pumpkin! I was about to call you. Have you landed yet?" Dillon asked. He was standing in the hallway of the Harris County courthouse, taking advantage of the ten minute recess.

"Not yet. About fifteen more minutes. We just crossed the Sabine River. We're over Louisiana now."

"Good girl, aware of your surroundings. I taught you well. I'm glad you called, I'm already missing you. The house is always so quiet without you."

"Dad, you've got Buster to keep you company. If you get...hey, wait a minute. There's a bunch of soccer players in the back that are making a lot of noise and I can barely hear you." Cassie looked back. "Okay, I think they've settled down. What I was saying...if you get really bored, you can always come visit me in NOLA."

"That's what I wanted to talk to you about. I was thinking about taking a short vacation and heading your way for some fishing. I'm about to wrap up a case at work. I could rent a boat and we could go out fishing like we used to when you were little and—"

"Dad! I'm not little anymore, and it's not the same without Mom. Put Buster in a kennel, I'll make you a hotel reservation nearby, and we'll go eat in the French Quarter somewhere."

"You know I don't like putting Buster in a kennel."

"Then bring him along. I'll make sure the hotel accepts pets."

"I'll think about that, and we'll talk later." Dillon paused. "Good timing on your call because I was about to call you and tell you something."

"What?"

"I'm about to win the big case! The verdict was being read a few minutes ago when the defendant started a fight, and the judge called a short recess. I know it...can feel it that the clerk was going to announce guilty."

"Really? That's awesome! Congratulations. I've been reading about the trial in the papers. Well, maybe not the paper but on the internet. The guy's from New Orleans, right?"

"Yes. Not for long. He'll be in a Texas jail soon, so it won't really matter where he's from. We got 'em, though. We made a deal with one of the gang members getting him to turn state's evidence in exchange for immunity and the witness protection plan. No honor among thieves anymore," Dillon said.

"Still, Dad, be careful. What was his name?" Cassie asked, snapping her fingers.

"Cole Cassel."

"I saw his picture online and he looks like a bad dude."

"He's not that tough."

"Hey, getting back to your trip—"

"Ma'am," a woman's voice said sharply.

Cassie looked up at the flight attendant standing in the aisle, arms crossed, with a Texas sized scowl on her face.

"Yes?" Cassie said, her voice barely audible.

"Your phone," she motioned. "We're descending so turn off your phone off and put it away." When Cassie didn't answer, the flight attendant said, "I'm not giving you a second warning. If I tell you again you'll be arrested when we land."

"Okay, okay," Cassie mumbled. "I'm talking to my dad. Let me say goodbye to him."

"Ma'am," the flight attendant said more sternly.

"I have to go, Dad. We'll talk more when you get home tonight, and we'll make plans to—"

The plane lurched violently!

Unprepared for the sudden heave of the plane, Cassie was forcibly rocked in her seat, and fortunately for her since she had tightened the seatbelt, she was kept her from being thrown out of it.

The iPhone flew out of Cassie's hand, hit the back of the seat in front of her, then lodged under her backpack.

The overhead lights flickered and went dark.

Someone screamed.

Complimentary drinks spilled, ice rolled on the floor. Luggage fell out of an unsecured overhead compartment.

Ryan lurched forward and banged his head on the tray on the seat in front of him. A gash opened on his head and blood trickled down the side of his face.

During the next few seconds, the plane dropped the equivalent of a ten story building. Passengers jolted forward then collectively slammed back into their seats.

A sharp dive followed.

More screams.

After a few seconds of nail-biting tension, the plane leveled off.

"Oh, wow!" Cassie said. "What was that?"

"Probably turbulence or wind shear," Ryan said. "I don't think I want to repeat that anytime soon." He looked at Cassie and Vicky. "You ladies okay?"

"For a moment," Vicky gasped, "I thought we were goners." She took a deep breath.

"Don't worry," Cassie said, "everything will be okay. Try to relax." She patted Vicky's arm.

"No, there's something wrong, the plane doesn't feel right. Oh my God, I don't want to die here." Vicky buried her head in her hands.

"Really, you've got to calm down. Try to think positive thoughts. We've only got a few more minutes and we'll be landing. Can you do that?"

Vicky gave a slight nod of her head.

"We'll go get gumbo after this, and—"

"Be quiet. Listen," Ryan interrupted.

"To what?" Vicky asked in annoyance. "I don't hear anything."

"That's my point," Ryan said.

Without the roar of the engines, the plane was eerily quiet. Only the low murmurings of the passengers and the rush of air gliding over the wings could be heard.

"What's wrong?" Vicky asked.

"I don't know," Cassie said. She looked around pensively. "It's too quiet," she whispered. "Oh, God. I think the engines have died." She put a hand to her mouth. "Ryan, have the engines died?"

"I think so."

"What? That's not possible." Vicky craned her neck, looking out the side window. "You're right. The engines! There's no sound! We're going to crash!" Vicky screamed. "We're all going to die!" She dug her nails into Cassie's arm.

"Calm down," Cassie said, trying to peel Vicky's fingers from her arm. She wasn't so sure her friend wasn't right. Cassie looked nervously around, waiting for instructions from one of the flight attendants.

A woman in front of her started weeping. A man dressed in a suit got out of his seat, opened the overhead bin, and retrieved a backpack.

Another passenger prayed audibly.

More weeping.

"Stay calm," Ryan said. "Don't panic. We'll be okay."

A thousand thoughts went through Cassie's mind at warp speed. What was wrong with the plane? Were they going to crash land. Would she survive? What would her dad do?

Dad!

She forgot to tell him she was okay. Cassie scanned for her phone, found it, and brought it up to her ear. "Dad? Are you still there?" Cassie waited for a response. "Dad?" Her voice was desperate. Taking the phone away from her ear she looked at the screen. It was black. She pressed the home button several times.

Nothing.

Still black.

"The phone's not working." She looked at Ryan. "What's happening?"

"I don't know. Make sure your seatbelt is on tight." He reached over and tightened Cassie's seat belt. "There, that's about tight as I can get it."

Cassie stuffed the phone in the back pocket of her jeans. Craning her neck she peered out the window. Murky bayous snaked across the land like a squiggly line a child had drawn. Pockets of marsh grass popped up, a flock of white egrets glided on a hot breeze. Cottony clouds floated, suspended in air. Cassie thought the scene looked deceptively tranquil and—

The plane took another dive, lost more altitude, and Cassie put a hand on the seat in front of her. Feet planted on the floor, she sat stiff-backed, the force pushing her into the seat. Her stomach was almost to her throat.

Frightened beyond belief, Vicky trembled, her eyes wide open. She grabbed Cassie's arm, holding it tight.

Adrenaline was pumping so fast through Cassie, she didn't feel Vicky's fingernails digging into her arm.

The plane shook and shuddered, sending violent vibrations along the fuselage.

Cassie bounced, keeping to the rhythm of the disabled plane.

Vicky hyperventilated, the back of her head mashed into the head rest mumbling, "We're going to crash. We're going to crash."

Think! Cassie's mind spun trying to think what she could do. The book! What had her dad said? *Count the rows to the nearest exit.*

"Put your head down between your knees, and put your arms over your head," Ryan said. "Prepare for a crash landing."

A chorus of flight attendants shouted, "Brace! Brace! Brace!"

Cassie did as she was told, put her head down, and wrenched her arm away from Vicky.

Seconds that seemed like hours passed, the plane torpedoing to the ground.

Count the rows to the nearest exit.

Cassie popped her head up and scanned the plane's exits, surmising the closest exit was three rows back.

"When the plane crashes, get out of the plane as fast

as you can. Go to the exit behind us. It's three rows back," Cassie said to both Ryan and Vicky.

"What?" Vicky whimpered. "Oh my God it's about to happen. We're going to die. We're going to crash!" Terrified and panicking, Vicky unbuckled her seatbelt and stood up. "I have to get out of here."

"Stop!" Cassie screamed. "Get back in your seat!" She struggled with Vicky, trying to force her back into her seat. "Sit down, now!" Once Cassie managed to get Vicky to sit down, she helped her with the seatbelt. "Remember, three rows. Once the plane has come to a stop, count three rows and run!" Cassie shook Vicky. "Can you do that?"

"I'll try."

"Get your head down!"

The plane vibrated so violently, Cassie thought it would disintegrate in mid-air. Something slapped the belly of the plane, hard. Terrified screams followed.

Ryan said, "Keep breathing."

Cassie tilted her head to the side, catching glimpses of the land. Patches of green whizzed by, trees, swatches of murky water, swaying marsh grass. Closer the ground came, and Cassie steeled herself for the inevitable.

There was a violent shudder then a foreign creaking sound of metal bending and twisting.

Sitting stiff-backed, her hands gripping the hand rests, Cassie lowered her head and prepared for the worst.

Chapter 4

"Cassie? *Calista?*" Dillon yelled into the phone. "Are you there? Can you hear me?" He paused and waited for an answer, perplexed regarding the strange noises he heard. "If you can still hear me I've decided to visit you next week. Okay? Call me back if you can in the next few minutes. The judge called a short recess."

He looked at the dark phone and cursed under his breath at the amount of dropped calls. Next week, he'd sign up for another cell phone provider.

Dillon put the phone in the inside pocket of his jacket and tugged on his tie. The damn thing felt like it was choking him. As Assistant District Attorney, he was required to dress a certain way for high profile cases. His suit was starting to feel mighty claustrophobic and he couldn't wait to get home, throw on some jogging clothes, and hit the trail with Buster.

At 5'9", Dillon wasn't much of a long distance runner, but what he lacked in height, he made up for in muscle. He had a low center of gravity, legs like tree trunks, arms called big guns, and an impressive set of pecs.

He had been a standout high school running back

and was slated for a big scholarship when he blew out his knee during his senior year in high school. Fast forward four years when he met Amy during college, married her, and a few years later he had a baby to support. Duty called, though, and he joined the military. There were bad guys to take down, and Dillon was the man for the job because he never shied away from responsibilities or controversies.

Getting back to civilian life was a challenge, and he found it difficult to get a good job until he decided to go back to school to get a law degree. Amy supported his decision and they made it through. Dillon worked odd jobs during the day, and at night, he went to school.

After a brief stint researching cases for a big law firm, he decided to do something more meaningful. Taking down bad guys was the thing for him to do. If he couldn't do it with brawn, he'd do it with his brain.

Years went by, Cassie grew up, and as future empty nesters, Dillon and Amy were planning for an early retirement, deciding to leave the fast lane for a slower pace. Plans were coming along and life was looking good until Amy died suddenly of a brain aneurism.

He had become a widower and an empty nester all within the span of a few months. He dreaded going home to an empty house. At least he had Buster.

Dillon headed back to the courtroom as the lights in the courthouse hallway flickered and went off. He stopped and looked around, waiting for the lights to come back on. These things happened all the time and he was used to it.

"Mr. Stockdale, come quick!"

Dillon turned around. It was the bailiff, Marcus Williams.

The big guy, close to retirement age, was a fixture at the courthouse. Normally he was all business with a baritone voice that was deep and steady. Dillon sensed

34

something was seriously wrong by the tone of Marcus's voice tinged with a quaver he hadn't detected before.

"The elevator is stuck, and people are yelling for help. I think we've lost power."

"Elevators have a backup system, right?" Dillon asked.

"Not sure. This building is as old as the hills and I don't trust these elevators."

Dillon silently agreed. It was one of the reasons he was in good shape. He chose to walk up and down four flights of stairs several times a day instead of trusting the elevators. The time he was stuck in one of them when it dropped a floor gave him the willies thinking about it.

"Come on," Dillon said. "Let's see what we can do." Dillon sprinted down the shiny marble floors leading to the elevator, Marcus racing right behind him.

Dillon pressed the call buttons several times and waited for them to light up. People were milling about in the hallway, some looking at their cell phones, while others were huddled around the windows. Dillon pressed his ear to the elevator door, straining to listen.

"We're stuck!" a muffled voice yelled. "Can anybody hear us? Get us out of here!" The voice echoed in the elevator tunnel.

Dillon shouted into the space where the elevator doors came together. "Hang on. Don't move." He turned his attention to Marcus. "Do you have anything we can use to pry open these doors with?"

"Don't think so," Marcus said, thinking. "Maybe you can use my baton?"

"Worth a try," Dillon said. He shrugged off his jacket and handed it to Marcus. "Hold this for a second."

"Help!" the voice echoed from inside the elevator shaft. "Help us!"

"We're coming!" Dillon yelled back.

"I can call maintenance..." Marcus stopped in mid-sentence realizing his phone didn't work either. He jerked his head to the people milling around the window. "Maybe someone over there has something we could use. In the meantime, see if my baton will work."

He handed the baton to Dillon, who immediately tried prying open the elevator doors.

A few strides later, Marcus came up to the window. Towering over the people, he glanced at the scene unfolding: Cars and trucks on the freeway had stopped moving. A motorcyclist had pushed his bike to the side of the freeway. Eighteen wheelers had stalled too, which was strange because it wasn't like it was a pileup and the traffic was bumper to bumper.

It was like they had all glided to a coast and stopped.

People had gotten out of their cars or trucks and were milling around. In the middle of the freeway, an old 1974 Gran Torino sputtered along like nothing had happened. Marcus recognized the car because he used to drive one.

"Something weird is going on," Marcus commented to nobody in particular. He ran to the opposite side of the hall to the view overlooking downtown. The scene was the same on the street grid. Buses, cars, delivery trucks, all stopped. Traffic lights had gone black. "Hey, Dillon, come see—"

Marcus was interrupted in mid-sentence when a collective gasp came from the people gawking around the window. He turned just as a woman broke from the crowd and raced to the opposite side of the hallway. Prospective jurors, attorneys, visitors, scattered like children's jacks being thrown on a slick floor.

Someone dropped a folder and an older woman stumbled and fell down.

Inside the courtroom, the occupants oblivious to the commotion in the hallway, Holly Hudson decided to take a break, too and check on why the lights were still out.

She left Cole Cassel strict instructions not to move a muscle. He huffed his understanding, all the while formulating his escape plan.

Holly strolled down the narrow isle of the courtroom, pulled out her cell phone, and using her shoulder she pushed open the door. Without looking up, she swiped the lock bar and proceeded to punch in the code when her concentration was interrupted as a man ran past her, almost knocking her down.

"Hey! Watch where you're going." Holly scowled at the man she recognized as a juror.

"Get away from the windows!" another juror yelled. He bolted past her, screaming, "Take the stairs!"

Holly's first instinct was to run, recalling what her daddy had said about his time working as a roughneck on an oil rig. *If you see someone running, don't stop to ask what for. You run as if your life depends on it.*

"Dillon? What's going on? Why is everybody running?" Holly asked.

"I'm not sure."

The expression on the jury foreman's face was pure terror. "The plane! It's heading straight for us! It's 9/11 all over again!"

Chapter 5

The 737 shuddered violently.

Cassie had her head down between her knees, hands clasped behind her head. Her teeth clattered. The plane was going too fast this close to the ground, and the wind pummeled the plane, rocking it wildly.

The belly of the plane was so close to the ground, Cassie swore she could smell the swamp.

The plane dropped further, clipping a massive five hundred year old oak tree, shearing off a branch like it was a piece of brittle uncooked spaghetti.

Treetops slapped the smooth underbelly.

Marsh grass swayed and whipped in the hot backflow.

The nose of the plane hit the ground first, tearing the cockpit off. It rocketed across the swamp, gouging the land like a plow over soft dirt.

The plane somersaulted once, effortlessly. A wing sheared off, spilling fuel.

A row of seats along with the belted passengers was torn out and heaved into air.

A detached bloody arm with a recent manicure of

shiny blue nails flew about the cabin. The fingers were still curled like a claw as if its owner had been clutching at something. The arm slammed into the roof of the cabin and left a bloody smear.

Cassie felt neither panic nor dread, and she let her body flow with the movement of the plane. It was like her consciousness had disconnected from her body, and she watched in suspended animation at the terror unfolding around her.

There was no fear. No dread. No screams—only the surreal sound of metal creaking and bending as the plane disintegrated into a metal pretzel.

Then it stopped.

When Cassie came to, she opened her eyes and took a difficult breath. She had no idea how long she had been unconscious. A plethora of wires and jagged pieces of metal appeared where the cabin had met the fuselage.

The air inside the cabin looked gray. Particles of insulation and carpet exploded when the fuselage was ripped apart. Lavatory doors hung open. Blue toilet water dripped into the aisle.

It was quiet sans the mutterings of the plane, moaning like a surgery patient fighting for consciousness after an operation.

When the carnage came to an end, Cassie sat stunned in her seat, still belted in. She brushed away the hair in her eyes trying to make sense out of the scene. The ceiling of the plane should be above her, yet all she saw was a crystalline blue sky with wispy cirrus clouds ribboning the horizon.

A marshy breeze came through carrying a salty scent. A heron flew by, wings flapping slowly, and Cassie followed the flight of the bird, mesmerized at the simplicity.

A jumbled heap of personal effects, a dented laptop, purses, clothes, blankets, a drink cart, and what looked to be pieces of bodies were scattered about the plane. Cassie couldn't understand why there wasn't a ceiling.

She looked to her right where Vicky should have been sitting. There was a hole in the side of the airplane, and Vicky's window seat was gone.

For a moment Cassie couldn't understand the meaning of the empty space where her friend since elementary school had been sitting. Then it dawned on her what had happened.

Dread welled up in her as she realized that if she hadn't let Vicky take the window seat, she would had been sucked out of the plane instead of Vicky. A shudder captured Cassie.

So, she was still alive. She forced herself to think, wondering what to do next. Injuries. Yes, that was it. Check if she was injured. She ran her hands over her arms and legs, feeling for injuries or broken bones. Putting a hand to her head, she felt a minor bump on her scalp. Her eyes could still focus, so a concussion was unlikely. Something was missing, though.

She couldn't understand the breeze brushing her face. She couldn't quite understand why there weren't any sirens screaming, or EMTs barking orders, or why she couldn't see any airport buildings.

"If anybody can hear me, release your seat belts and get out!" Cassie recognized the voice. It was Ryan, and a thought crossed Cassie's mind that he wasn't dead either.

Ryan screamed the orders again. "Release your seat belts and get out!" The order snapped Cassie out of her trance.

She reached to the seat belt and fumbled with it until it clicked open. She stumbled out of her seat.

Ryan rushed over to her. "Are you hurt?" His question was met by a blank stare so he repeated the question. "Are you hurt?"

"I don't think so." Cassie stood up, a little wobbly at first, her legs like rubber bands. Her jeans were torn, her dark green Tulane University t-shirt stained with someone else's blood. Her long brunette hair was a tangled mess. Fortunately, her tennis shoes were still on her feet.

"Let me help you," Ryan said. He put an arm around her waist. "Let's get out of here."

Exiting the wreckage, Cassie's eyes shifted from Ryan to the remnants of the plane. Only a few seats were intact, and when she scanned the cabin, there was no indication of a pattern or any reason why some seats were intact, while others weren't.

When she went to take another step, her shoe pushed down on something soft and wet. Looking down, she nearly jumped out of her skin. Cassie recognized the man as the guy sitting opposite her, one aisle in front. His eyes were open a slit, his mouth frozen as if he was about to ask a question. Blood soaked his chest.

"What's wrong with him?"

"There's nothing you can do for him. Leave him," Ryan said in a matter-of-fact tone.

"Is he dead?"

"Yes."

"How do you know?"

"Seen bodies like that at car crashes."

"Don't we need to cover him up?"

"No. There's nothing we can do."

"Where is everybody?" Cassie asked.

"I think we're it," Ryan said.

Chapter 6

Dillon grabbed Holly by the arm. "Ruuuun!"

The drawn-out scream sliced through the chaotic din. Holly didn't need to be told twice.

When Dillon and Holly turned to run, a loud explosion ripped through the courthouse and the force of the concussion knocked both of them off their feet, hurling them in different directions.

Dillon hit the floor, rolling like he was taught in football: tuck the knees in, arms bent and close to the chest, relax the legs. When he stopped rolling, he instinctively hunched his back and covered his head.

Having not been as lucky or possessing such quick reflexes, Holly was thrown against the wall, her head hitting a hard wooden railing, arms and legs flying in all directions. She crumpled to the floor.

Chunks of ceiling and concrete rained down. Dillon was pelted with plaster, covering his shirt and navy blue pants in a chalky white residue.

He lay on the floor, stunned, his ears ringing. When he came to his senses, he shook his head trying to clear the cobwebs. For a moment he thought a gas line had ruptured. All sorts of gray matter blew around—pulverized insulation, sheetrock, mortar, pieces of ceiling tiles, bricks reduced to powder, and whatever else made up the top floor.

Coughing, Dillon choked the gray dust matter out of his lungs and pushed up. He knelt on one knee, trying to make sense of what had happened.

Muffled cries of anguish and repentance, wives calling for their husbands, sons mumbling for their mothers filled the hallway.

"Marcus?" Dillon called. "Marcus can you hear me?" Dillon listened for a moment until he heard what he thought was a tornado, or what he thought one should sound like because he hadn't ever actually heard one. The Texas Gulf Coast rarely got tornadoes.

Another explosion rocked the building, followed by a deafening roar.

Dillon teetered on unsteady legs, unsure what to do. Squinting through the haze, his eyes followed sunbeams casting light on the hallway. Curiosity got the best of him and he stumbled over bodies and debris, making way to the window.

Black clouds of billowing smoke filled the sky, obstructing the view of what should have been the downtown skyline of magnificent architecture and shiny windows.

An enormous bowling ball of fire appeared instantaneously on the outside of the building. Like the power needed to throw an Olympic javelin, the fireball steamrolled the outside wall of the diminutive county courthouse.

Dillon didn't have time to process the inferno. He acted instinctively and hit the floor, sucked in a breath, and held it. He protected his head best he could, and put his back to the fiery assault. He counted, one one thousand two one thousand, three one thousand...

The fireball barreled down the hallway with the force of an out-of-control locomotive. Angry flames lashed at the walls, igniting anything flammable in its path, followed by a fiery *whoosh*.

Dillon kept counting, waiting for the searing heat to subside. Nine one thousand, ten one thousand. His heart beat faster, and when his lungs felt like they were about to explode, Dillon exhaled and gulped a big breath expecting air.

He gagged.

It was like his lungs were paralyzed, like he was scuba diving the time his equipment malfunctioned, when his air tank was empty.

Panic set in.

He knew he was commanding his body to breathe, but his lungs wouldn't work. He felt consciousness waning, and twinkling stars appeared in his vision.

He felt weak, this was it...

The fireball flamed out as it blew through a hole that used to be a window. A second later, oxygen-rich air gushed in, filling the room gloriously.

He gasped and coughed, willing his lungs to work.

A fire in the corner of the hallway was quickly extinguished when the gravity-fed sprinkler system automatically engaged. A jagged pipe spewed a forceful stream of water, drenching the survivors and what was left of the 4th floor of the county courthouse.

Rolling over onto his back, Dillon took stock of the carnage that was reminiscent of a war zone during his time in the Gulf War. He remembered survivors with singed hair and charred clothes poking their heads out of the rubble.

He remembered the sights and smells. People wandering aimlessly. The death and destruction.

This was war all over again.

The United States had been attacked.

He shook his head trying to clear his mind of the fuzzy images.

The building had a gaping hole in the ceiling, ragged and shell-shocked survivors milling around. Some were moaning, crying for help. Others were too still.

Dillon stood up and his right hand went to his hip, an automatic response, searching for his military-issued Beretta M9. It took him a moment to realize he was standing in the Harris County Courthouse in Houston, Texas instead of broken buildings of Fallujah, Iraq.

Dillon's training kicked in and he called out for the bailiff. "Marcus? Marcus!"

"You looking for the bailiff?" a shaky voice came from behind him.

"Yes," Dillon said. He whipped around and stared at the woman. He knew he should recognize her but the cobwebs in his brain made his thinking fuzzy.

She was sitting with her back against the wall cradling one of her arms, her legs stretched out in front of her, her new pantsuit ruined beyond repair. One of her pumps was missing. Her eyes peeked out of soot-covered skin, her shoulder length blonde hair previously tied in a smooth chignon now hanging about her face, matted with blood.

Dillon struggled to remember her name. He couldn't focus, and looked at her oddly. His head felt like a jar of marbles was bouncing around in it. Her face was familiar and the first name to come to him was Amy.

But Amy was his wife.

His deceased wife.

"Holly," she finally said. After a pause she continued, "Holly Hudson. Are you okay?"

Dillon put his hand to his forehead, feeling a knot.

"I don't know. I think so."

He shook his head, hoping to clear it. He remembered her clearly now.

She was forty-something, unmarried. He knew that because he'd checked out her ring finger that morning, somewhat pleased she wasn't wearing a band or diamond on her manicured nails. He briefly recalled feeling sheepish about his actions, hoping his inquisitiveness had gone unnoticed. Regardless of being adversaries in the courtroom, she was an attractive woman.

"I heard you calling for Marcus." Holly glanced nervously in the direction where Marcus was. "I don't think it's good."

Dillon turned in the direction Holly had nodded. Marcus was prone and unmoving, his face mashed into the floor. His khaki shirt was smoldering.

Dillon rushed over to Marcus, bent down, and held his index and middle fingers to Marcus' neck to check for a pulse.

Nothing.

He tried another spot for a pulse. Still nothing, not even a flicker. Dillon positioned his hands under Marcus, heaved, and when he turned Marcus over, it became apparent why there was no pulse.

A piece of shrapnel had been driven into Marcus' chest, leaving a gaping hole, probably killing him instantly. There was nothing Dillon could do.

"Dillon," Holly called. She held out a weary hand, motioning him to come over. "Can you help me?"

Leaving his friend, Dillon went to Holly. His training as a military medic kicked in and he visually made a quick check while his expert hands gently pivoted her head looking for injuries. Finding none, his hands made a sweep of her arms and legs, feeling for shrapnel. "Where are you hurt?"

"My arm hurts, and it's bleeding."

"Let me see."

Holly hesitated.

"I was a medic in Iraq. It's all right." Dillon gently straightened Holly's arm. As soon as Holly removed pressure, the three-inch gash started bleeding again. "It's not as bad as it looks. You'll live."

"You sure about that?"

"As of now, I'm not sure of much of anything. Do you have anything I can tie around your arm to stop the bleeding?"

"Would a scarf work?"

"Yes."

"There's one in my left pants pocket. You'll have to get it please. I can't move my arm."

Dillon reached over Holly and dug his hand in the pocket. It had been a long time since he had been this close to a woman. Longer since he had even entertained the thought of being near a woman. Not since his wife had died. He pushed those thoughts out of his mind and slid his hand deep in the pocket. Grabbing the scarf, he wrapped it around the wound. Coming to the end of the scarf, he used his teeth, ripped it about six inches down the middle, then tied it off.

"That scarf cost sixty dollars," Holly said.

"It's priceless now because it's going to save your life," Dillon said. "Keep steady pressure on the arm and don't move it. Can you do that?"

Holly nodded.

"Can you move your legs?"

"I think so."

"Good." Dillon hooked an arm around her waist and stood her up. "Start walking home."

She gave him a weird look and frowned. "Walk home? No way. I'm going to call 911 and have an ambulance take me to a hospital. I don't think I should drive."

"They won't be coming."

"What do you mean, *they won't be coming?*"

Dillon made a mental check of everything that had

happened. Lights had gone dark, phones weren't working, cars stalled except for an old 1970s vintage Gran Torino, traffic lights were dead, a plane had lost power, clipped the building, and crashed somewhere in downtown Houston. There were no sirens, the steady hum of the city had gone silent, and—

"My daughter," Dillon said. "Oh my God. I have to get to her. I have to leave. I'm sorry."

"Wait, what's going on?" Holly asked.

"I was on the phone with my daughter when... She was flying back to New Orleans when the phone went dead." Dillon hung his head and put his hand to his forehead. "I have to go to her."

"Catch the next flight. There's a flight every hour out of Hobby going to New Orleans."

"You don't understand," Dillon said gruffly. "Nothing works. There's no electricity, no phones, computers, cars, buses. Nothing."

"What are you talking about?" Holly asked.

"An EMP."

"An EM what?"

"Electromagnetic Pulse."

"What is that?"

"It's a bomb that has been detonated high above the United States somewhere. We learned about it in the military. In theory, the electromagnetic pulse fries everything that uses electricity. Anything that relies on a computer is toast. That's why the cars you see stalled on the streets looked like they coasted to a stop. The engines stopped working. That's why the plane fell out of the sky. That's why the lights went out and the phones don't work." He stopped for a moment letting Holly digest the information. "That's why nobody is coming for you. For anyone."

"That's impossible. If all that happened all at once, we'd be in a lot of trouble."

"Exactly."

Holly put her hand to her face. "I don't know what to do. I knew I should have gone back home instead of taking this case."

"Any family in town?"

"No."

"Friends?"

Holly shook her head. "I've worked so much these past few years, I haven't had time to make friends."

"Where are your parents?"

"Both deceased."

"I'm sorry to hear that." Dillon paused, thinking quickly. "We can't stay here. The building's not safe anymore. I'll help you out of the building then you can head home."

"It's really too far. I don't have any food. I just moved from an apartment to a house in the burbs and haven't even had time to go to the grocery store."

"Then you can come with me."

"What?"

"You can come with me or stay here and take your chances."

Holly gave him a blank look.

"Holly, society as we know it has come to an end."

Chapter 7

Cassie stumbled near the airplane wreckage, carefully picking her way around razor-sharp metal and pieces of bodies. Putting on mental blinders, she tried to focus her gaze straight ahead as she followed in Ryan's footsteps. Keeping her head down, she navigated the shallow murky waters and islands of swamp grass.

Cassie looked back at the remains of the 737. It looked smaller, lower, and the thought occurred to her that the swamp would swallow the plane.

For a few more treacherous yards, Cassie and Ryan sloshed through the swamp water. A water moccasin slithered out of the swamp grass, and Cassie stopped in her tracks.

The mid-October sun was hot, the humidity making it worse. A bead of sweat trickled down Cassie's back, staining her t-shirt.

A swarm of biting gnats swirled in the still air.

Considering a plane had crash landed, the lack of noise and activity was nerve-wracking. It wasn't like in the movies with explosions and sirens wailing or police and EMTs immediately coming on the scene. It was only her and Ryan. She'd die if he knew she had been fantasizing about him only an hour ago.

Cassie suddenly felt thirsty. A fly lighted on her forehead and she swished it away. The knee-high marsh grass swayed in the light breeze. A white egret glided effortlessly overhead, and a falcon searching for a meal cast an eerie shadow upon the land.

The flight of a turkey buzzard lifting off the gray bones of a long-dead oak interrupted her thoughts.

Something didn't feel right.

"Wait," she said. Ryan turned around. "Something's wrong here. We need to go back to the plane and try to find water and food."

"Let's keep moving because it's going to be dark soon. I don't want to be stuck out here at night."

"Exactly. We should go back and take shelter in the plane. It can get cold here at night and if our clothes get wet we could get hypothermia."

Ryan thought about what she said before he answered. "You're right. It *will* be dark soon and if we're stuck out here without any provisions, things could get ugly really fast. If I had my camping supplies it would be no big deal."

"Do you have anything in your backpack we can use?" Cassie asked.

"No, only some water. I packed my camping gear in my checked luggage which is probably somewhere at the bottom of the swamp."

"That's probably where mine is too. Damn. There was a lot in it."

"We can't be that far from I-10. I've flown this route so much I practically know it like the back of my hand," Ryan said.

"Do you see any roads? Hear any cars? If the interstate was that close we'd hear the road traffic," Cassie pointed out.

Ryan listened for a moment. "That's weird. I don't hear anything. You're right, let's head back."

An hour later, the sun was an orange saucer in the low sky. Clouds ribboned the horizon, bathing it in swirls of orange and blue hues. A bullfrog croaked in the distance, and somewhere a cricket chirped.

Cassie climbed back into an open section of the fuselage, avoiding the framework of beams exposed like the carcass of a butchered animal hanging in a meat shop. It might as well have been a meat shop because the plane felt like death.

It was too quiet, and everywhere she stepped, it was like she was in a cemetery trying not to walk directly over a grave. A body could be under the mound of debris, or a part of a body. Flies were buzzing all around, and Cassie knew what that meant.

A sudden chill captured her and she shivered in the warm evening.

Everywhere she stepped, personal belongings were scattered. Opening a carry-on bag, since she couldn't find her own, Cassie rummaged around in it. It felt like she was violating the person's belongings. Still, she forced herself to continue. She pulled out a dog-eared romance paperback, pair of tennis shoes, a change of clothes, and digging deeper she found a bottle of water, a package of crackers, and a candy bar. She tossed the book aside and zipped up the bag.

"Ryan?" Cassie yelled. "Have you found anything?"

"I found a couple of flashlights. You?"

"Some water and food, and a change of clothes. I'll keep looking. I'm trying to find the galley," Cassie said.

"Hey, I found some blankets. We'll need those tonight."

"Great."

Cassie continued searching for anything useful among the wreckage. There were several laptops, a camera, briefcases, a present wrapped in kid's wrapping paper. So many useless items. What they needed was food and water, and anything that might be used as a weapon.

This was the wilderness, and soon it would be dark.

Soon the scavengers would come out.

Chapter 8

"Come on," Dillon said. "We need to go. *Now.*" It was a terse order instead of a polite command. He was standing on the fourth floor of the Harris County Courthouse. He could have kicked himself for telling Holly she could come with him. Having to be responsible for someone else hadn't been in his plans. Especially a woman. Once he got home, he'd make her comfortable, check her arm, give her something to eat, then he'd be on his way. After that, she'd be on her own.

He had to find his daughter, and that was foremost on his mind.

Holly answered in an equally terse way. "Okay, I'm coming."

They navigated their way down the stairwell to the third floor, second floor, and finally the ground floor. They were awestruck at the scene they walked into.

The plane that had clipped the country courthouse had nosedived into an office building several blocks away, obliterating it, reducing it to a smoldering heap of rebar and chunks of concrete. Angry flames shot out of the rubble.

Blue-gray smoke billowed skyward forming a thundercloud of organic ashes of lost lives and unfilled dreams incinerated in the ugly din.

On the street, a few office workers wandered around in a daze, covered in a layer of dust.

Someone on a bicycle whizzed by, leaving a trail of dust. A homeless person stood on a street corner, begging for money from anyone walking by.

It was eerily quiet. The steady hum of downtown life had fallen silent. Buses had coasted to a halt, the beep-beep of car horns nonexistent, no sound of tires upon concrete.

"What is that smell?" Holly asked, wrinkling her nose. She couldn't quite place the putrid odor. "It smells like some sort of meat that has fallen through the grill onto coals."

"I think that about sums it up," Dillon said.

It took a moment for that realization to sink in. "Oh," was all Holly said. She put her hand to her cheek. "Those poor people. Do you think anyone survived that?" Holly asked, pointing to the rubble.

"Let's hope not."

"Kinda harsh aren't you?"

"I can only hope that the people died instantly without suffering. If they are trapped they'll die slowly, because no help is coming."

"Of course help will come," Holly countered. "How can you be so mean?"

Dillon ignored her question. "See any fire trucks or ambulances? Hear any sirens?"

Holly scanned the streets in all directions. "Not yet."

"Like I told you," Dillon said, "society as we know it has changed. Have you tried your phone lately?"

Holly gave him a blank stare.

"Go ahead. Try it."

Holly pulled her cell phone out of her pocket and

pressed the home button. When nothing happened, she pressed the on/off button and waited. Still nothing. "Maybe it's broken." She shook it, as if rattling the insides would make it work.

"It's not broken and shaking it won't help. It won't work regardless of how many times you try. Anything with a circuit board will not work, and probably won't for the foreseeable future."

"I can't believe that," Holly protested. "This is the 21st century. There are safeguards."

"You're wrong this time, counselor," Dillon said. "Our fancy law degrees are worthless. You can object all you want to, but as of now, it's the law of the jungle. The strong will survive. Those that prepared and have stocked up on food and weapons will survive. That homeless guy you see over there," Dillon said, pointing to the street corner, "he'll probably live because he knows how to scavenge. He knows how to make a fire, how to make a shelter out of plastic and cardboard. He can boil water to drink. That man over there, the one with the three piece suit and shiny loafers? He will probably starve to death in a matter of months. It'll be the sick that will die first. Medicines will run out. Antibiotics won't be manufactured anymore and anyone with a serious infection or illness will die."

"So what you're telling me is that the end of the world starts at the corner of Franklin and San Jacinto in downtown Houston?"

"That's about right."

"I can't believe it."

"Believe it."

Holly's thoughts went to her bleeding arm and what Dillon had said earlier. "What about me? I mean my arm. Are people like me going to die?"

"When we get to my house, I'll take a look at it." He made direct eye contact with Holly. "As of now, we're on our own. We'll need to live by our wits and help ourselves because no help is coming for anyone." He squeezed her good arm. "Listen to me. The police will be useless because they'll be helping their families first."

"That's not right," Holly protested.

"Maybe not." Dillon shrugged nonchalantly. He took her by the elbow and shuffled her along. "It's what happens during catastrophes. Look what happened during Hurricane Katrina and all those people stranded at the Superdome in New Orleans. Something like 15,000 people. You saw the pictures on TV, right? The dead were left where they fell. People slept in urine. Water was rationed to two bottles a day per adult. Toilets stopped working for thousands of people. Can you imagine what a city of a million people will be like after a week without power or infrastructure?

Holly didn't answer.

"It's going to be a hellhole," Dillon said. "The aftermath of Katrina happened because the government was too slow. They had to assess the situation and make a plan, have meetings, talk about it, and have conferences calls and other bullshit, and that was all using high tech communication. There's no communication now, so don't plan on the police or government helping us. We're going to have to help ourselves. We've talked enough, so let's get going now. I've got a lot of stuff to do. I'm leaving tomorrow to go find my daughter. I've got to get her back home."

"You said she was on a plane to New Orleans. If everything with a computer has stopped working..."Holly stopped in mid-sentence and glanced down.

Dillon stared hard at her. His words were careful when he said, "She should be okay. She has to be. Tomorrow, I'm going to go find her."

Dillon wasn't able to admit that his daughter's plane

would be dead in the air when the EMP hit. Call it self-preservation, or having his head in the sand, he couldn't yet go to that place thinking his daughter was dead. He wouldn't.

He couldn't.

It would kill him.

Chapter 9

Cassie shivered in the damp swamp air. With her knees bent and her arms wrapped around them, she huddled under a piece of the airplane that she was unable to identify in the low light.

"Here," Ryan said, "take another blanket."

"Thanks." Cassie took the thin gray blanket, shook it open, and wrapped it around her shoulders then tucked it up to her chin. "Have you seen any suitcases? Maybe we could find a jacket in one of them."

"I've already looked. Can't find any. I'm guessing the cargo hold was ripped open some ways back and all the luggage fell out."

"So much for my plan of dressing for the night out," Cassie said.

Ryan laughed. The humor seemed to alleviate their dire situation.

"How much daylight do you think we have left?" Cassie asked.

Ryan peered at the sun sliding beneath the horizon. "Maybe half an hour."

"I haven't seen any search planes. Don't you think

they've started searching for us?"

"I don't know. I guess it will take them time to coordinate a rescue effort. Right now, they should be mapping the flight path and calculating the probable crash site. The plane is a thousand more times visible from the sky than a single person is. Don't worry," Ryan said, "I'm sure we'll be rescued by noon tomorrow."

Ryan didn't say his statement with resolve. He had also noticed the lack of activity in the air, not even a prop plane, helicopter, or a jet trail high in the atmosphere. There wasn't any boat activity either, and he knew from his days as a biology major at Louisiana State University this area was prime real estate for alligator hunting. He'd keep that little bit of knowledge to himself while he kept an eye out for the apex predators, the telltale sign of rippling water, a splash, or if he had a flashlight, glowing beady eyes bobbing above the waterline. He'd seen that in Florida and the thought they were being watched sent shivers up his spine.

"You're cold too?" Cassie asked. She had noticed him shiver.

"Not too much."

Arms tucked close to her body, Cassie briskly rubbed them, trying to get circulation going. She wiggled her cold toes. "It's so cold."

"It's the dampness that makes it that way," Ryan said. He stood up and stamped his feet. "Ever been to Colorado?"

"Once, when I was a kid. Why?"

"It can be freezing with snow on the ground, and it doesn't feel as cold as it is now because it's so dry there. Here when it's cold the humidity sucks all the warmth out of you. I'm guessing the temperature is around 65 degrees, but the humidity makes it feel like 50."

"Where exactly do you think we are?" Cassie asked.

Ryan paused, thinking. "Probably in the southern

part of the Atchafalaya Basin."

"A nice word for a swamp," Cassie said. She put a hand to her face. "Shit."

"What?" Ryan asked.

"You know how big the Atchafalaya Basin is?"

"Yeah. About half the size of Rhode Island."

"We're fucked," Cassie said.

"No we're not," Ryan said. "Look, all domestic flights are tracked on radar, so once our plane disappeared that would have been noted. The last known location will give a good idea on where the search can start. It'll be better in the morning."

"Well, maybe so. What I wouldn't do for a cup of hot chocolate and a fire."

"I don't think a fire would be a good idea with all the spilled fuel," Ryan said. "But I could make you a cold hot chocolate. I spotted what's left of the galley about a hundred yards from here. And I've got an extra bottle of water."

Ryan's nurturing gesture took Cassie by surprise. "Sure, that would be nice."

"I'll be back in a few minutes. It's getting dark. I'll be in hollering distance, so if anything happens, just yell."

Cassie tracked Ryan until he became a small dot. It was eerily quiet sans the low whisperings of the wind and the creaking of shifting metal. Sitting alone, it was frankly quite unnerving. Growing up in the city, Cassie was accustomed to the steady hum of activity and the comforting sounds of life. In her apartment near the French Quarter, she'd listen to the street life, people walking and talking, the sounds of traffic, the hustle of street vendors, music. Cassie sought out quiet places, and even though solitude invigorated her, right now she was scared out of her wits.

Her senses were attuned to the night, and sounds were magnified. The wind might as well have been a tornado.

With so many dead bodies around, it was like the essence of the deceased was still here, the night air thick with lost lives. The thought of being in a cemetery was terrifying, not that the dead could hurt anyone, but in the silence Cassie's mind played tricks on her.

A movement and a loud splash in the marsh caught her eye and she turned that way. Squinting, she tried to understand the hazy images.

Moonlight shimmered on the water, and Cassie stared sightlessly out over the dark land and swamp. The Atchafalaya Basin wasn't a swamp in the true sense of the word, more like a mixture of swamp and bottomland. It contained hardwoods, bayous, and backwater lakes. The significant part was forest habitat, while the smaller part was populated by marsh and open water. The plane had crash landed on the fringe of the forest habitat, the home to the Louisiana black bear, a fact unknown to Cassie and Ryan.

The wind had picked up and Cassie thought she saw movement in the marsh.

Some night animal scurried nearby, rustling the grass and leaves. Spooked by the unknown sounds, she jerked her head to the side, her eyes wide with fear. There was more movement, then another noise she couldn't discern. It sounded like someone moaning. Cassie couldn't be sure, chalking up the sounds to an overactive imagination. That and the fact she had recently watched the latest slasher movie didn't do her any good. She really hated those movies, but Vicky loved them and had talked her into it.

Vicky, she thought.

Cassie dropped her chin and rubbed her forehead, wondering whether or not to tell Vicky's parents the truth about how their daughter died. That if Vicky hadn't insisted on the window seat, their daughter would still be alive. She'd wrestle with that decision at a later date. She swallowed hard.

A flight of a night heron broke the spooky silence and Cassie looked skyward trying to find the large bird. A frog croaked, then more joined in on the amphibian orchestra until the air was filled with different levels of bellowing baritones.

Listening intently, she filtered out the swamp sounds. Then she heard *that* sound again.

Considering it was dark and the noises of the Atchafalaya Basin swamp were surprisingly loud, Cassie chalked up the noise to her overzealous imagination. The screech owl sounded more like a woman screaming, and the croaking frogs more like a jackhammer on the water. The sounds were magnified only by the imaginings of what could be making them.

She really wished Ryan would come back.

Chapter 10

When Dillon and Holly came to the entrance of the parking lot, he said, "I need to stop by my car."

She gave him a questioning look. "What for? You said cars don't work."

"They don't," Dillon answered curtly. "I need to get my..."

"Get what?"

"Equipment. Look, my car is on the tenth floor. Are you up to climbing ten flights?"

"I think so."

Dillon's eyes dropped to Holly's feet. "Are you okay to walk? You only have one shoe."

"I'll make myself okay."

"Good. How's your arm holding up?"

"Good enough. It still hurts, though."

"If you need any stitches, I'll put them in when we get home."

"Stiches?" Holly's tone was one of surprise.

"Yes."

"Using what?"

"Needle and thread."

She gave him a strange look.

"Pretend you're a pioneer woman."

"You've got to be kidding me."

"I'm not kidding. I can stitch it up. Done it before under much worse conditions. Come on, let's get going."

Dillon took the stairs two at a time, barely breaking a sweat, an easy feat considering he was in shape. Holly followed behind, mirroring his steps, although she climbed one stair at a time instead of two. The higher she went, the dizzier she became. At the landing of the fifth floor, Holly's thigh muscles burned and started cramping.

"Wait," Holly said. She leaned against the concrete side and sucked in a big breath of air, her heart thumping hard against her chest. "Go on without me."

"I don't think it's safe for you to stay here by yourself. I'll wait until you catch your breath."

"No really, go on. I'll sit here. I'm feeling a little dizzy that's all." Holly rubbed her arm. "I think it's bleeding again."

"Let me look at it," Dillon said. He untied the scarf he had used as a tourniquet, trying not to get his hands bloody. He peeled back the blood-soaked scarf, now stuck to her arm. He grimaced at the sight and swore under his breath. The wound squirted a little blood each time Holly's heart beat. "Yeah, this will definitely need some stitches," he said, tying the scarf back around her arm tightly. "Try to stay still and concentrate on lowering your heart rate. The slower your heart beats, the less you'll bleed. And don't talk to anybody. I'll be back in a few minutes."

"You sound like my father."

"I'll take that as a compliment because I am a father."

Leaving Holly alone, Dillon breezed the next five floors, although by the tenth floor, he was feeling the effects of climbing ten flights of stairs, not to mention the near death experience he just had. The adrenaline that had kept him jacked up had finally waned, and now his own injuries were starting to hurt.

His shoulder, which still had shrapnel in it from his time in Iraq, was tingling and throbbing like someone had whacked him with a piece of rebar. It brought back unwanted flashes of bloody battles. Dillon's mind wandered to the horrific wounds he'd treated and the men he couldn't save. As a medic, he saw the worst of war. He thought he had put those mental wounds to bed, but when his body hurt, those memories came flooding back.

Sprinting to his car, he weaved in and around the parked vehicles, cursing that he had chosen a parking space on the opposite side of the stairwell. A couple of people milled around near their cars, dumbfounded as to what to do.

As Dillon ran, his thoughts went to Amy, his late wife. She had helped him come to terms with his time in Iraq, and had saved him from being a broken man. Amy was gone now, and Dillon had been forced to become both mother and father to Cassie during the two years since his wife had died.

After the death of his wife, Dillon had thrown himself into his work with a newfound determination to put away as many criminals as possible. That's what he kept telling himself. He couldn't face the fact he had become a workaholic to fill the emptiness he felt. The house was so quiet without Amy. There was something comforting when he drove up to the house after a day's work, knowing someone was listening for the patter of his footsteps. The only one listening for him now was Buster, a once cute 10 pound ball of wiggly fur, a "gift" Cassie had given him after Amy died.

His daughter had said, "He'll keep you company, and

a reason to get up in the morning, if only to let him outside." The 10 pound wiggly ball of fur had grown into 70 pounds of hound dog.

Leaving a dog alone for most of the day hadn't been the best of ideas. After coming home day after day to torn and soiled carpet, Dillon had installed a doggie door so Buster could let himself outside when needed. Apparently the dog much preferred the sofa in a temperature controlled environment to a sunny spot outside because whenever Dillon came home, Buster was inside waiting for him.

Now that he thought about it, having a dog did fill some sort of longing or need.

Dillon had other things on his mind, too, like the latest trial. It was a minor victory among all the current carnage. Fortunately, the jurors had seen through all the lies and were about to hand down a guilty verdict on that lousy piece of shit who thought he could strut into Houston and claim it as his own. Maybe the plane did everyone a favor by dispatching Cole Cassel, though Dillon wasn't sure what had happened to the guy. Last he saw Cassel was sitting at the defense table, chatting with a groupie like nothing had happened. These types of trials brought out all sorts of people.

Coming to his old car, Dillon stopped, swiveled around, and said, "Shit!" He palmed his head. How was he going to find his daughter? The realization hit him that Cassie's plane had probably gone down somewhere in the vast and dangerous expanse of the Atchafalaya Basin, a 260,000 acre mix of swamp and forest. It was home to the Louisiana black bear, monster alligators, and nearly impenetrable wetlands.

He said a silent prayer in the hopes the Almighty would hear him, granting him this one request to keep his daughter safe until he could reach her. It was the first time he had said a prayer since Amy had died. None of his prayers had been answered in the hospital where he had kept a vigil, waiting for Amy to regain consciousness. She never had. Now, for some reason, he felt a little better acknowledging his troubles to a higher authority.

He couldn't bring himself to go to that dark place to face the reality the plane Cassie was on would have crash landed. He couldn't think of her not surviving a plane crash. He couldn't bear to lose his only child, not after his wife was gone. His daughter was the reason for his purpose in life. If the pilots were any good, or had any military training, they could glide the plane as far as possible before landing hard. It was a scenario they should have been tested on in flight simulators, or at least he hoped so.

He held onto that thought.

To find her, or the plane, he'd have to do a quick calculation of where the plane was when the EMP struck. It would be a crude calculation, based on the departure time and approximate speed, and now that he thought about it, he remembered the flight attendant giving her a hard time about being on the phone. So, the plane must have begun descending.

Standing at his car, which was a relic of the 80s, he pointed the key fob at the car, and beeped it open. Fortunately, battery operated devices without a computer board still worked.

Dillon wasn't the kind of guy to buy the latest car with all the bells and whistles. This one worked well enough to his satisfaction with an AC, radio, and a CD player. Change the oil every few thousand miles. Besides, it had been paid off years ago, leaving him plenty of leeway to put his money in things that he would need now. Things that would sustain his life.

Fishing around in the glove compartment, he found a faded Texas/Louisiana map. Folding it, he stuffed it in his pants. Following the little blue dot on the map app on his iPhone would be useless in his upcoming travels. He'd have to skirt I-10, the main interstate connecting Texas to Louisiana and eastward through other southern states. Instead he planned to stay in the shadows and follow the rarely used farm-to-market roads of the East Texas Piney Woods.

He was home in that country.

Nobody would guess he had a semi-automatic AK-47 in the trunk, not in a jalopy like this. The AK was his go-to rifle. A reliable weapon, it wouldn't jam in wet or sandy environments, and rarely wore out. It could be dropped, used as a club or a cane without sustaining any serious damage. That and the fact it was simple to operate made it one of his all-time favorite guns. He could overlook the fact it was only effective to about 300 yards. What hunter shoots a deer at 300 yards? Probably not many.

He swung around to the trunk, pushed in the latch, and the trunk popped open. Quickly, he retrieved a backpack. Standing at the back of the car, he checked his surroundings making sure he was alone. Light was fading fast, and the open air garage wouldn't be a good place to be after dark. As soon as the sun went down, looters would come out as sure as thick green scum forms on a stagnant pond smothering the life out of it.

Dillon loosened his thick leather belt and slipped the Kydex holster in place. He buckled back up. With his elbows tucked close to his body, he held the Glock 17 9 mm pistol securely, right hand on the grip, index finger resting outside the trigger guard, left hand cupping the right one. Always a stickler for safety, he squinted, racked the slide back, and peered into the chamber. A round was already chambered. Having an extra round in addition to the ones in the magazine was comforting. Seventeen rounds plus one in the chamber equaled eighteen chances to stay alive.

He placed the Glock in the holster then grabbed a couple of magazines and secured those in the pouch also on his belt. Dillon was one to be prepared, knowing two extra magazines were better than one. Tugging his shirt out of his pants, he covered the Glock with his shirttail.

Time to hoof it.

With his AK slung over his shoulder, he padded down the stairwell of the garage and came to the floor above where he left Holly. He stopped dead in his tracks. The hair on the back of his neck stood up, and that gut feeling he'd had so many times in Iraq spoke loud and clear.

It's that little voice that says *stop, something's not right.*

That sixth sense early humans relied on to survive against larger predators. The predators in today's urban jungle weren't as big but were just as deadly, and Dillon proceeded with caution.

He exhaled slowly and pressed his back into the shadows of the concrete wall. Deftly, he unholstered his Glock, holding it in both hands.

He listened intently, trying to filter the extraneous sounds. A benign conversation drifted down from one of the upper garage floors. There was laughter and some more conversation. A car door thumped shut. Footsteps upon concrete.

All normal.

Nothing to worry about.

Directing his hearing to another location, it was the muffled angry voices with an unmistakable accent that caught his attention.

One voice he recognized.

He strained, trying to catch a word or phrase. A flight of pigeons spooked Dillon, and he flinched at the sudden movement.

It was then a scream so shrill, so viscerally frightened, sliced the air.

He recognized it, too.

Holly.

Chapter 11

Dillon faced a serious decision. If he left now, he'd have a chance to find his daughter because he'd still be alive. His daughter would definitely need him. Or he could try to save Holly. However, if he was wounded or worse, he'd never be able to help his daughter or know what happened to her.

On the other hand, if he left Holly to the unpleasant fate that was sure to befall her, he wouldn't be able to live with himself. He was that kind of a standup guy. He was the guy who had your back in an alley; the kind of guy that looked out for the little guy; the kind of guy that wouldn't leave a lady, even if the lady was one he had a contentious relationship with.

Shit.

There really had only ever been one decision.

Dillon thought quickly about the best offense. In the close quarters of the stairwell, the AK wouldn't work because he could accidentally shoot Holly. Fortunately, his Glock loaded with hollow points would do the trick because once the bullet hit flesh, it would expand instead of exiting the body. Less chance of collateral damage.

He inched his way down a few steps, and the voices surrounding Holly were becoming more ominous with each passing second.

Dillon heard three distinct voices. Two were unidentifiable, while the third belonged to Cole Cassel. He strained to listen to the conversation, waiting for the moment he'd make his entrance.

He steeled his nerves, raised his Glock to firing position, and took a big breath. The element of a surprise attack would be his best offense.

He'd shoot first and ask questions later.

"Looky what we got here, boys," Cole Cassel said.

Holly closed her eyes and turned her head, recoiling from Cole's hot breath on her neck.

"Hmm? No quick retort or objection, Ms. Defense Lawyer? Or is it Mrs. by now?" Cole's tone was mocking. "Hey boys, I think we got a women's libber on our hands." Cole's groupies from the trial laughed. "You've been making me answer all your stupid questions and sit nicely like I'm some goody two shoes choir boy, and what did I get for it? Probably a guilty verdict. Now you know I don't like losin' one bit. I paid you mighty handsome for you to get me off. Good thing the plane came to my rescue, and if you think anyone is coming to *your* rescue, like the bailiff, you'd better think again. That stiff won't do you no good no more," he said, running his hands through Holly's hair. "Brings back good memories. Don't it?"

Holly recoiled from his touch and closed her eyes.

"Remember what I said would happen if you didn't win my case?" He held a lock of her hair to his nose and sniffed.

Holly didn't answer.

"Hmm?"

Holly winced and thought quickly while Cole pawed

her and driveled on about what he was going to do to her. While he inspected her tattered suit, she sneered at his cohorts and refused to show fear. She had managed to scream before Cole had stuck a knife to her throat telling her if she screamed once more, he'd slice that tender white throat of hers from ear to ear.

If Dillon was the kind of man she thought he was, he wouldn't leave her. And if he had his wits about him he probably should be somewhere close by, possibly even listening. He'd be armed too, or she hoped he would be. He didn't exactly say what he needed in his car, but she took an educated guess, being aware of his military background.

That's right, she had done her own intel on her courtroom adversary, knowing that Dillon had done a stint in the military, been wounded, and had come home, married, had a child, and gone back to school.

Though she knew he was a widower, that didn't garner him any slack in the courtroom. She was a fierce competitor and knowing her adversary was a way to win.

She scanned her surroundings checking for any indication Dillon was near. Maybe a shadow where one shouldn't be, or a bird whistle among birds that weren't song birds. The only clue he might be around was the spooked pigeons that suddenly scattered.

Maybe he *was* close.

All her senses were heightened and her heart beat fast, her mouth dry.

"I think it's time you answer some of *my* questions," Cole taunted. "Still got that nice spread in East Texas. Barn too? As I recall your daddy liked his guns. Now where do you suppose all of them went to? Got a secret hiding place? Fake wall or something? I've heard 'bout people making safe rooms."

Holly didn't hear what he had said after that because she was attuned to her environment. Cole was behind her while the two other jokers flanked her. She wanted to give Dillon a clean shot at Cole, but she couldn't manage to position her body in a way it would be possible. With the two guys on either side, at least Dillon could get them.

"I got myself an idea, boys. Let's write up a bill of sale right here. I'll title it 'Land for your life'." Cole jabbed the handle of his knife into Holly's wounded arm.

Holly flinched and let out a wounded scream, piercing the stairwell.

"Got your attention, finally," Cole said. "Anybody got a pen?"

"I do," one of the groupies said, handing it to Cole.

Cole took the pen and put it in his shirt pocket. "You know the old saying business before pleasure? I don't really cotton to that. Let's have pleasure before business." He took the knife and flicked off the top button of Holly's silk shirt. "Well, boys, why don't we show Ms. Defense Lawyer what she's been missing?

Holly refused to beg but she could barter, stalling for time. "Cole, I've got money. I can go to the bank and withdraw a couple of thousand for you. Cash. No questions asked. You can—"

The first round caught the guy to Holly's left in the throat and he stumbled back, dropping to the floor. Blood squirted on the walls of the stairwell. He grabbed his obliterated throat and flailed around like a fish on a dock trying to escape a filleting knife.

The second round cracked bones and ribs of the next guy, and the 9 mm hollow point sent him to an early and quick death when his heart exploded. He crumpled to the ground, a stiff spasm capturing his body before he went limp. He still had a surprised look on his face when the lights went out.

Dillon swiveled the Glock a fraction, trying to sight in on Cassel.

Coward, he thought.

Cassel was using Holly as a human shield, and the third shot Dillon knew would be a whole lot trickier because Cole had Holly in a chokehold with the knife pressing into her throat.

"Drop your gun or I swear to God I'll slit her throat," Cole ordered. He pressed the knife harder into Holly's neck. Holly stood frozen, afraid to exhale. "Do it! Now!" He was cornered like a rabbit with no place to run, and was about as frightened. His bravado leaked out as fast as the blood on the dead goons' bodies.

Holly had her fingers wrapped around Cole's forearm, willing Dillon with her eyes to do something.

Dillon's gaze swiveled from Holly to Cole. He gambled that Cole wasn't willing to die to exact revenge on Holly. With hawkish eyes, he stared laser straight at Cole. "I'll never give up my weapon. Maybe you'll slit her throat, and maybe she'll die. If she does, you'll be next, and that's a guarantee," he said, his voice steady and low.

A shout echoed through the garage momentarily distracting Cole and his eyes flicked that way.

Holly sensed the distraction, and with great determination she raised her foot, using the heel of her remaining pump to slam it back into Cole's shin.

The shearing pain reverberating along his leg caught Cole by surprise. He grunted and instinctively flung Holly toward Dillon.

In the close quarters, her off-balance momentum caused Dillon to waver a second before he caught her with his left hand. By then, Cole had escaped through the doorway leading to the landing then to the next flight of stairs. Beyond that was the alley behind the garage. Cole hobbled to the corner, favoring his throbbing shin, all the while looking back, checking if Dillon was following. A few more yards and he'd be on the banks of Buffalo Bayou. From there, he could disappear in the tangled brush and gnarled trees lining the bayou.

Dillon still held the Glock in his right hand. "Are you okay?" he asked. "Did he hurt you?"

"You bastard!" Holly spat. "You took a gamble on my life. I can't believe you would do that."

"Guys like Cole are basically cowards. He wasn't about to die for you. He's like a rat that jumps ship when it is going down, and he knew he was about to go down." Dillon touched her chin, moving it gently, inspecting her for any new wounds. "Are you hurt?"

"A little shaken up but I'm okay."

"Good. Stay here. I'm going after Cassel."

"No," Holly pleaded. She put a hand on his arm. Dillon looked down at her hand and Holly, acutely aware she was touching him, abruptly removed her hand. "Don't leave me again. I've got a bullseye on me now. Not everyone likes defense attorneys, especially ones who don't win the case for their clients. There's no telling how many other prisoners have escaped."

"I thought you only took white collar crimes."

"I *had* to take this one," Holly said.

"Why?"

"Never mind," Holly said tersely.

Dillon really wanted to ask what she meant by that and what Cole had meant when he asked *Still got that nice spread in East Texas?* but decided against it. Holding his Glock in both hands, he popped his head out the doorway. "I have to go after him. He's dangerous. I'll be back in a second."

Holly opened her mouth to protest but couldn't muster the strength. She slid down and sat on the concrete floor, resting her back against the wall. "Do what you have to do. I'm not going anywhere."

Dillon sprinted down the stairs. After a quick jaunt to

the end of the garage, Dillon's suspicions were confirmed. Tracks in the soil led from the garage to the bayou.

He followed the tracks halfway down the grassy embankment. It was obvious the person who left them had been running. Dillon scanned the thick tangle of brush and trees. It would be impossible, if not foolish, to try to track Cole any further. This part of the bayou leading out to the ship channel was a virtual river city of homeless people, prostitution, and drug users. Trash and drug paraphernalia were scattered around. Empty liquor bottles littered the area. The people living on the fringes of society had claimed possession of the bayou a long time ago, making it a dangerous place at night.

Coming back to Holly, he said, "He's gone now, probably trying to cross the bayou. Good riddance. Maybe the current will get him. It's not as tranquil as it looks."

"That doesn't make me feel any better. He could be back because he's a survivor."

"I doubt it," Dillon said. He put a hand under Holly to help her up. "It'll be dark soon, so we need to get going."

Rising, the blood drained out of Holly's face and she looked at him with a strange expression. Wobbling on unsteady legs, her eyes rolled back into her head, and she crumpled like a puppet whose strings had been cut.

Dillon reached to catch her before she fell and hurt herself any more. Holding her, she weighed more than he originally estimated. Deadweight always felt heavier. He heaved her up, positioned her sideways across his shoulders, one arm over a thigh, the over latched onto an arm, carrying her like an injured soldier.

An AK on one shoulder, a woman draped over him. If Dillon had been younger, this would have been his dream. As it was, he had 120 pounds of deadweight to carry, all shit had broken out, and he was looking at a

long five mile trek to his house. On foot.
Fucking great.

Chapter 12

Dillon carefully wove his way down the next few flights of stairs and when he reached the bottom, he checked both directions. A grim office worker passed by him, glanced briefly at the woman he was carrying, then proceeded on without asking questions or offering help.

This was the first sign of how it was going to be. Dillon had seen that look of desperation before; how people measured the cost of helping versus the return they would get. He had seen it in the villagers of Iraq, doors closing that time when he had barely escaped a firefight, carrying a wounded soldier, desperately searching for a safe place. Knocking on doors, only to be met by angry shouts and clubs.

It was only one life to save, but one life counted for something, especially to the family. It mattered to Dillon, like the life of Holly mattered. To someone hopefully in *her* family.

Holly and Dillon had been adversaries in the courtroom, exchanging barbs, and he didn't know much about her personally other than she had a sharp wit and was the consummate professional. Tough as nails wouldn't aptly describe her tenacity when it came to winning. He supposed for a woman to get ahead in a man's world she had to be tough, otherwise she'd get eaten alive in the dog eat dog world of the legal system.

Maybe that was why their professional relationship was strained, he pondered. It was because she was a lot like him. Amy, on the other hand, had been the powder to his primer, the .22 to his .44, complementing his shortcomings, and he hers. Now that he thought about it, any of her shortcomings were minor compared to his. She made him realize life was a journey and that winning wasn't everything.

The long hours he put in as an assistant district attorney had become weary and right before the aneurism that claimed Amy's life, they had made a decision to sell their house and to visit a rural community where they could buy a piece of property, grow vegetables and fruit trees.

He wanted to learn husbandry so they could be self sufficient in case there ever was a worst case scenario. The only thing he hadn't planned on was it happening so soon.

After Amy died, Dillon felt empty, like his life had no meaning. His daughter had grown up and had left home to begin her own life. He hadn't even entertained the idea of dating or marrying again. Amy had been his soulmate, each of them finishing the sentences of the other.

Maybe this was the jolt he needed to put things in perspective, and with society breaking down, he could become whatever he wanted to.

He had skills others didn't, and his survival training would come in handy now. He had an impressive stockpile of weapons and ammo, food and water. He could live off the land if needed. He could hunt and fish. His bugout bag was ready.

He plodded on, carrying Holly, his legs starting to burn at the extra weight on his shoulders.

Getting back to the problem at hand, he contemplated what to do about Holly. Once she woke, he'd tend to her injuries, get her stable, then ask her to leave. Come morning, he'd start out for New Orleans.

He found it odd she didn't show any fear when Cole had a knife to her throat.

Could she had known he was close enough to help her? How did she know he was armed?

To kick the asshole in the shin required guts. Had she done it to help Dillon, or was it a desperate tactic of someone close to dying who had no clue about hostage situations?

Now that he thought about it, a crack in that porcelain veneer had appeared after Holly crumpled in his arms. She was human after all.

Maybe there was more to Holly Hudson than met the eye, though she *was* easy on the eyes, Dillon had to admit. Thinking about Holly in that way surprised him because it had been a long time since he had thought about another woman. He had other things on his mind at the moment, so he pushed those thoughts aside.

He had to get home.

Chapter 13

The trek from the courthouse to his home had been uneventful. Oh sure, he had gotten the evil eye from some of the more unsavory types that lurked on the outskirts of downtown, but once he showed the AK, the thugs backed off.

A little firepower went a long way.

Holly had been passed out the entire time. Although she moaned and uttered something which sounded like she was talking in tongues, other than that, she hadn't been a problem.

He had crossed under the I-10 interstate where it cut through the center of town within the 610 Loop. He was now on his home turf, Heights Boulevard, and he walked a few more blocks to a side street where his house was located. It had been built in the early 1900s, having seen better days before he and Amy bought it. Amy had done a good job scavenging estate sales looking for furniture and anything else they needed, drove a hard bargain on repairs, and over time had made the house into a home. Dillon never really appreciated it until after Amy had died. It didn't feel the same, or welcoming.

83

The house was dark, and when he opened the squeaky front gate Buster started barking. Walking up to the porch, he turned when a voice called, "Dillon?"

Dillon recognized the voice belonging to his neighbor, Larry Williams.

"Do you need some help?" Larry asked. He craned his head looking at the woman draped over Dillon's shoulders.

"Yeah. Can you open the door for me?" Stooped over from carrying Holly for the last hour, Dillon fished around in his pocket and handed his house keys to Larry.

Larry took the keys and opened the door.

Buster came barreling out, all 70 pounds of slobber and barks, and he wiggled all over, stamping his feet on the porch, welcoming his owner. Moving his head side to side, Buster's nose worked to identify the person standing next to Dillon. Buster barked his curiosity until he recognized the man as the next door neighbor. Buster sidled up to Larry and nosed him until a hand patted his head.

"Man, that dog's big!" Larry exclaimed.

"When my daughter got him, he was a puppy, about a tenth the size he is now. We didn't know he'd get so big," Dillon said. "Buster, go on and do your business."

As if understanding the verbal clue, Buster loped off the porch and went to the yard.

"Who is that?" Larry asked, pointing to Holly.

"A colleague."

"Hmm." Larry scratched the stubble on his chin, studying Dillon. "You look like you got hit by a car."

"Actually a plane."

"What? No shit. *A plane?* You gotta be kidding."

Dillon pushed forward, heading down the hallway. "A plane hit the courthouse this afternoon."

"So what happened?"

"Larry," Dillon said, "I'm too tired to go into right now. This lady needs help."

Larry didn't acknowledge the last statement. "That explains the explosion I heard. I was in my Lay-z-Boy watching TV when all of a sudden, boom!" Larry made an exaggerated motion with his hands. "The house shook and a few seconds later the electricity went out. I've been trying to call the electric company for hours but the phones are out too. And now there's a bunch of stalled cars on the street. What's going on?"

Dillon didn't have the heart or the energy to tell Larry what was really going on. Larry was one of those neighbors that always seemed to be either outside when Dillon came home, or in the front room watching TV so he could keep an eye out for anybody coming or going. Dillon thought he should be glad Larry was his neighbor because Larry was a built-in free burglar alarm system. The guy had eyes in the back of his head.

"I don't really know what's going on," Dillon said. Coming to Cassie's room, he pushed the door open using his foot. Larry was right behind him, and if he had been a herding dog, Larry would have been nipping at Dillon's heels.

"So why'd you bring your colleague home instead of going to the hospital?"

"Look, Larry, I don't have time to go into all the details. Let's just say things aren't going to be the same for a while."

"What things?" Larry asked.

"Everything."

Larry gave him a confused look.

Dillon paused. "I'm tired and I've been carrying this lady for a long time. I need to get her on the bed. Do me a big favor and get me a towel and some water. Wet it down a little but not too much."

"You want me to boil the water? Like they do in the

movies?"

"Cooktop won't be working. Tap water will do for now." Dillon placed Holly on the bed.

"Okay, on it."

"Get Buster back in and shut the front door too, will ya?"

"Sure thing."

Dillon tried to make Holly as comfortable as he could. He took off her remaining pump and set it on the floor. He lifted her head and positioned a pillow so she wouldn't have any pressure on her neck, then covered her with a blanket.

She was breathing evenly, so Dillon surmised she must have passed out from the overwhelming events.

He walked into the kitchen and retrieved a flashlight. Dillon was a stickler for changing out batteries in all his flashlights. The batteries got old after a while, sometimes bursting, and one thing Dillion didn't like was a ruined flashlight. He had the flashlights color coded with stick-on dots, coordinating the colors with the seasons, so he'd remember when the batteries had been changed out. Blue was for winter, pink for spring, yellow for summer, and red for fall.

It was dark in the house and Dillon clicked the flashlight on and walked back to Holly. Her color was still good, and he checked the bandage on her arm. It was holding up, though he'd have to change it soon. The pressure had staunched the flow of blood for now. He'd suture it later. Walking to the bathroom, Dillon said, "Hey, Larry, never mind. She's sleeping now."

"Oh," he said, looking like a deer in the headlights. "What do you want me to do with the towel?"

"Hang it up to dry."

"Okay," Larry said. "You look like you're about to pass out. Can I do anything for you?"

A long sigh escaped Dillon's lips. He leaned into the

wall. If he stayed there any longer, he'd fall asleep standing up. "As a matter of fact, yes. Got anything to eat?"

"Louise made a chicken casserole before we lost electricity. Want some of that?"

"Sure."

"Give me a few minutes and I'll be right back. Do you want Louise to come over and have a look at..." Larry paused looking at the bed.

"Her name's Holly."

"Oh, right. Louise could come over in case Holly needs some female..." Larry paused, clearing his throat, "you know... *things.*"

Dillon had lived long enough with his wife and daughter to be used to whatever female *things* Larry was talking about. Besides the female *things*, Dillon hadn't even cleared out Amy's toiletries. He still had her hairbrush and makeup, along with her clothes and shoes. When he really felt down, he'd open her favorite perfume and remember...

"Tell Louise thank you very much for the casserole. Holly will be okay here."

Larry shrugged. "Back in a jiffy."

Dillon escorted Larry to the door and told him that everything would be okay. Buster squeezed in and made a beeline to the kitchen.

"You hungry?" Dillon asked.

Buster's eyes were big and round and he had that look on his face when he was ready to eat, which was about anytime of the day. That dog could eat an impressive amount of dog food.

"Here ya go," Dillon said, setting down a big bowl of dog food.

While Buster wolfed down the food, Dillon pondered over what to do with him. Maybe he could talk Larry into taking care of Buster. Nah, that wouldn't work because Larry had a yappy little dog and a cat that made Buster nervous. They might end up being snacks, like the squirrels had been. Not really a snack, more like a present Buster offered Dillon when he came home from work. Many times Dillon had been greeted by a dead, chewed on squirrel that had been left on the front porch. For a big dog, Buster could move with the agility of a cat.

Option two was to leave a big package of dog food in the kitchen for Buster, prop the doors open so he could come and go as he pleased. Dillon surmised he would be gone a week, two at the max, so Buster would be okay until he got back.

He could fill every bowl in the house with water, and when it rained, the water would replenish the lily pad pond in the backyard. Dillon had built the pond especially for Amy and they'd sit in the lawn chairs in the backyard, watching the minnows swim around.

There was still so much of her in the house. Everywhere, even the smallest trinket reminded him of a memory.

He took a couple of his favorite LED lanterns, flipped the on switches, and placed one in the kitchen and one outside Cassie's bedroom door. He preferred LED to incandescent bulbs because LEDs required a lot less electricity, not to mention they were shockproof if dropped.

Walking back into the kitchen he opened the dark and somewhat cold refrigerator, feeling around for a beer. When he found one he popped off the lid and took a big pull. He savored the moment, knowing it would be a long time before he had another cold beer.

A few minutes later Larry came back carrying a Tupperware container with two servings of the chicken casserole, a roll with butter, and green beans. Buster followed Larry around, his nose in the air, following the scent of food.

"He acts like he hasn't eaten in a week," Larry said.

Dillon laughed. "He's always like that. Thanks for the food."

"Sure, no problem. Least I can do" Larry said. "So tell me about what's going on. Louise is worried that the phones still don't work."

"How much non-perishable food do you have?" Dillon asked.

"Like canned goods?"

"Yes."

"I don't know, maybe a few weeks. Louise gets mad at me if I buy too many canned goods. You know, money's tight and all. Why do you ask?"

"I've got to leave first thing in the morning, and I'll be gone a while. If you run low on food, you have permission to use whatever I have. Here," Dillon said, "follow me."

Dillon motioned for Larry follow him to what used to be a bedroom. Opening the door, he shined a flashlight on what could double as a small, fully stocked grocery store. There were shelves and shelves of all sorts of canned goods covering every item in the food pyramid. One wall contained canned fruit and vegetables, canned tomatoes and spaghetti sauce; another wall had flour and pasta, and a separate one for canned meat. A smaller shelf contained medical supplies and ointments.

"What the hell?" Larry exclaimed. His eyes roamed wherever the flashlight beam illuminated. "You stocking up for the apocalypse?"

"Something like that. If you get hungry, use whatever you need. Also," Dillon said, leaning into Larry, "this is important. Don't tell *anybody*. Do you understand? You're probably going to need this."

Larry indicated his skepticism and replied, "Sure. Whatever. I've heard about you guys. Preppers. Isn't that the term? Macho kind of guys, right?" Larry said, knuckle punching Dillon in the arm. "So why'd you ask me if I had any food when you have all this?"

"I like Louise's home cooked food. Thought it would be a while before I get any more."

"Nah," Larry scoffed. "Electricity will be back on by morning. You'll see."

"I doubt it. Believe me, one day soon, you're gonna be real happy I stocked up like this." Dillon motioned to the front door. "I've had a really long day and I've got a lot of things to do. Do you mind?"

"Oh, sure. Time for me to get back home. What are you going to do about Holly?"

Chapter 14

Good question, Dillon thought. He was so consumed with fatigue and memories of Amy, he had forgotten about the wounded woman in the next room.

"She may stay here for a while," Dillon said. "I'll see how she is in the morning."

"Call me, or rather, yell if you need anything," Larry said.

After Larry left, Dillon devoured a helping of chicken casserole, ate the roll, and half of the green beans. He covered the other half and put it in the refrigerator, which would keep the food cold for a little while longer. If Holly was hungry when she woke up, she could eat that.

Turning around he was surprised to see Holly. "I thought you were still sleeping."

"I heard you talking so decided to get up."

"Want anything to eat?"

"No really. What I need is a stiff drink."

"Bourbon and seven?"

Holly nodded.

Dillon made Holly's drink, stirred in a couple of

melting ice cubes, and handed it to her. She took it, her hands shaking so much the ice cubes clinked around the glass.

"Are you okay?" Dillon asked.

"No. I can't stop shaking." Holly leaned on the kitchen counter and took several big gulps until the drink was gone. "I can't believe what has happened, especially how Cole cornered me in the garage. He probably would have raped or killed me. I can't believe he would do that."

"You say that as if you know him."

Holly didn't reply. She lowered her gaze then sucked down the remaining bourbon. "I need another drink."

Dillon took the bottle of bourbon and splashed in another couple of ounces. "Here," he said, "this should help. Want any more Seven-Up?"

Holly shook her head, downing the drink in one big gulp. She set the glass on the counter. "Everything we've worked for and the life we've built. Gone, simply gone. I don't know what to do, or who to turn to. I'm sorry I passed out on you. Sorry about what I said to you in the stairwell. I'm sorry I'm a burden to you." Her chin dipped and she burst out in tears.

Dillon patted her on the shoulder. "Don't cry. You're not a burden. It'll be okay."

"No it won't." She stifled a sob and wiped the back of her hand across both cheeks.

Dillon tore off a paper towel from the dispenser and handed it to her.

Holly wadded the paper towel and wiped her face. She sniffled and took a couple of big gulps of air. "I can't believe all those people in the building died. I mean, one minute we are all looking at our text messages, the next a plane obliterates the building."

Holly paused and took several breaths of air. She swallowed hard. "And to think Marcus was months away

92

from retiring. I can't get that image of him laying dead on the floor out of my mind. Oh, God, his wife doesn't even know, and—" She burst out crying, covering her face.

"Don't cry," Dillon mumbled.

"—and Marcus was taking care of two grandkids that still depend on him."

"They'll be okay. Please don't cry."

"I can't stop."

"Try. Crying isn't doing you any good."

Holly nodded then burst out crying again.

Dillon shook his head. "Come on now. You'll be okay." He took a step toward her and put a hand on her shoulder. Patting her shoulder he said, "You're going to be okay."

"How can anything be okay again?"

"It just will. There, there," he said.

"Okay," Holly sniffled.

"You're here with me. We've got food. Heck, I've even got an entire cabinet of good booze, so it you want to get shit-faced you can. I've even got a dog you can pet. And there's left over chicken casserole in the fridge, which you need to eat tonight."

Holly gulped a big breath of air. She took the paper towel and patted her cheeks again. Her shoulders dropped, her head went limp, and she rested her head against Dillon's chest.

Dillon moved his hands to the back of her head, slowly brushing her hair then encasing the back of her neck. Holly leaned into him and put a hand on his back.

"It'll be okay," he said again, stroking her hair. "It'll be okay, you'll see." He pulled her closer, letting his hands drop to her upper back. He stroked her back through the thin shirt. Holly hiccupped. "Shh, it'll be okay." His hand slid further down to the curve on her back and stayed there.

Neither one breathed or moved, and after several seconds of utter silence, Holly leaned her head back.

Dillon met her gaze, looked into her deep blue eyes and thought, *Oh shit.*

Chapter 15

Sifting through the remnants of the galley, Ryan scavenged two cans of Coke, four bottles of airplane bourbon, several packs of peanuts and pretzels. When it became too dark to continue he stuffed the items in his backpack, slung it over his back, and sprinted back to the crash site, water and mud splattering his jeans.

Taking the blankets and pillows Cassie had found, they huddled together in what was left of the section of plane they had been seated in before the crash. A damp swamp breeze whistled through the plane, and the smell of petrol permeated the air.

The scavenged food made for a very meager late dinner, while the bourbon took the edge off their anxiety. They had savored the drinks and snacks, taking an hour to eat.

The taxing events of the day mentally and physically exhausted Ryan and Cassie, and after they ate, both dozed off.

Cassie woke to a cold breeze brushing over her and the sounds of the swamp. Frogs croaked, one at first, others joining in from what seemed like miles around. It was incredibly loud and Cassie shivered.

"Are you awake?" she asked.

"Yes," Ryan replied.

"Why is it so loud?"

"It's always loud in the wilderness at night."

"How do you know?"

"I camp a lot."

"Where?"

"All over the place. This time last night, I was sleeping under a West Texas sky."

"Tell me about it," Cassie said.

"Big Bend National Park is beautiful. It's a place where you can get away from it all. It's quiet and peaceful. Food tastes better. The stars are bright, the night air crisp. Last night I stayed awake looking at the sky waiting for a streaking star."

"Do you ever see any?"

"Quite a few, actually."

"Did you make a wish when you saw one?"

"Why? Is this truth or dare?" Ryan asked.

"No," Cassie said. "Trying to make conversation. I'm not used to it being so dark."

"In that case," Ryan said, "what do you wish for?"

"I asked first."

"That you did." Ryan pondered for a moment before answering. "Winning the lottery."

"I'm serious," Cassie said. "What do you wish for?"

Ryan shifted in his seat. "This is making me uncomfortable."

"Me or the question?" Cassie asked.

Ryan didn't answer.

"Then I'll go first," Cassie said. "I wish for a home and a husband, kids and a dog. And a long happy life."

"Sounds like the American dream."

"Maybe so. Your turn now," Cassie said.

Ryan took a deep breath. "Much like yours. A bunch

of kids, four maybe, because with three someone is always the third wheel."

Cassie laughed at that. "Why not three? Were there three kids in your family?"

"No," Ryan said. There was a hint of sadness in his voice. "I was an only child. My parents were old when I came along. I always wished I had a brother, and I was envious of guys who did. With a brother, you've got a built in lifelong friend."

"I was an only child too," Cassie said. "It didn't matter because me and my mom were best friends."

"I'll get you back to your mom," Ryan said.

"She's deceased."

"Oh, I'm sorry to hear that. Both my parents are gone too."

Cassie put her hand on his arm. "I'm sorry. It must be hard on you not to have any family."

Ryan turned his head and met her caring eyes. She didn't know the half of it, and he found himself really wanting to tell her more, that he always felt the odd kid out and not quite belonging. His adoptive parents were great, but he always had a longing to know his birth parents. At this moment all he wanted to do was to kiss Cassie and take her in his arms, this girl who was strong. She had survived a plane crash, was level headed, and he admired her for that. As he looked at her, he realized she was more of a young woman, someone he really wanted to know better, to protect her. The more he looked at her, the more he wanted to kiss her. He thought she must have felt it too because she held his gaze. It wouldn't seem right, not here, not this moment, so he fought the urge and turned away.

Cassie removed her hand and sighed. After a few uncomfortable moments of silence she said, "I really need to pee." Rising from the seat, Cassie stepped over Ryan and into the aisle.

"Don't go too far," Ryan said. "And don't step out of the plane. It's too dark and no telling what's out there."

"I won't go very far, only past the front rows. So don't look."

Ryan huffed. "I won't."

Cassie shuffled her feet, pushing away any debris that might trip her up. Keeping her hands on the aisle seat, she counted seven rows.

"That's far enough," Ryan called.

Cassie turned so that she was facing Ryan's direction. Dark or not, she didn't want to take a chance on mooning him. She fumbled with the button on her pants and unzipped them. Groping around, she found a seat tray to hold onto so she could keep her balance. After she did her business, she breathed a sigh of relief and stood up. The creaking noises the plane unnerved her and she heard *that* sound again. Something akin to moaning garnered her attention. Telling herself it was only her imagination in overdrive, she took a step but her leg wouldn't move forward. Jerking it, she thought her pants leg had gotten caught on a piece of metal. When she jerked again something grabbed her leg.

Her immediate action was to kick to wrench her leg away. Fear in her rose and she kicked harder at whatever it was holding onto her leg.

"Ryan! RYAN!"

"What?"

"Help me! Something's got my leg."

Ryan catapulted from his seat and bolted to her.

Cassie struggled to free her leg.

"I can't get it to come loose," she said. "Do something!"

It was so dark Ryan couldn't see her tennis shoes, so he gingerly ran his hand down her leg feeling for the object holding her back. Expecting to find metal Ryan jerked his hand back when he touched something warm that moved.

"What is it?" Cassie asked.

"I don't know," Ryan said.

"Hurry up because whatever it is I think it's moving."

"Shh, quiet. I thought I heard something." With great trepidation, Ryan followed the contour of Cassie's leg until he came to the bottom of her pants. His fingers tentatively explored the area, and when his hand found the object holding her leg he immediately knew what it was.

"Help me," a gravelly voice croaked.

Cassie jumped.

"Help me," the voice said again.

"Oh my God! Somebody is alive."

"We're here and we're going to help you," Ryan said. "You need to let go."

After the shock of finding another passenger alive, Ryan and Cassie took action. Cassie remembered that she had a mini light on her key ring, so she sparingly used the light so Ryan could free the man.

It turned out his name was James Morley, a lawn mower sales executive who was on his way to Atlanta for a convention.

Using a makeshift lever, Ryan lifted a piece of the airplane off of the man while Cassie pulled him free. Much to everyone's surprise, James stood up. He was wobbly so Ryan told him to sit down while he gave him a cursory examination using the light on Cassie's key chain. From what he determined, James only had a nasty bump on his head. He had been knocked cold, didn't remember anything about the crash, and was shocked to hear that most everyone had died.

"You mean we are the only ones that survived?" James was flabbergasted only three people out of all the passengers and crew had lived.

"We're it, unless we find someone else in the

morning. Unless they are uninjured, which I don't think is possible, there's nothing we can do for them," Ryan explained.

"What caused the crash?" James asked.

"Don't know," Ryan said. "Probably a catastrophic engine failure or something worse."

James rubbed his head. "How long has it been since we crashed?"

"Probably about eight hours," Ryan said.

"That's long enough for the authorities to launch a search. I'm guessing since the plane was late, there'll be rescue planes looking for us. The black box has a transponder on it, so they'll be able to find us. Have you tried calling 911?"

"Our phones aren't working."

"Oh," James said, "I guess there aren't any cell towers in the middle of the swamp."

"That's not what I mean," Ryan said. "Our phones are dead. They won't turn on."

"I'll try mine," James said. He patted his back pants pocket feeling for his phone. "Still got mine." Taking it out, he clicked the home button waiting for it to light up. Nothing happened, so he tried again. Turned it off and on. Still nothing. "That's odd. Mine isn't working either. Guess we'll have wait for someone to find us."

"Yeah, well," Ryan muttered, "you can stay here if you want to, but we plan to save ourselves. Right, Cassie?"

"Right," she responded.

"What are you talking about?" James asked.

"We are going to walk out of here," Ryan said.

"Are you crazy?" James asked. "You can't just walk out of here."

"We can, and we will," Ryan said. "We leave first thing in the morning. You can come with us or take your chances here. The decision is yours."

Chapter 16

Dillon figured it was about 1 a.m. Holly had fallen fast asleep after their unexpected romp in the hay, and was now snoring lightly. Dillon had been awake the whole time thinking *What the hell have I done?* He was so wired up he couldn't even keep his eyes closed. If he had a time machine like Marty McFly had in *Back to the Future*, Dillon would have used it and when she had looked at him with those puppy dog eyes, he would have told her to take a cold shower. Jesus! What was he thinking? Bedding his colleague?

There was no undoing what they had done, and since he couldn't sleep he decided to get up and pack.

He headed to the hall closet, taking out the suitcases and sundry other belongings until he uncovered his bugout bag. He heaved it out and took it to the living room. Placing it on the floor, he unzipped it and took out all the contents. He had purchased the items over several years, discarding some and buying others depending on sales and what he thought he might need.

Studying it, he decided it needed to lighten the load. He tossed the radio, crowbar, and bolt cutter first. A couple of things he could wear on his backpack, such as the Nalgene water bottle, so he kept that. Extra ammo and a knife could go on his belt, while the Camelbak would go in the hidden pocket in the pack. He kept the Lifestraw and water purification tablets, protein bars, matches, first aid kit, flashlights, duct tape, paracord, and contractor trash bags. If he needed shelter in a hurry, he could fashion one out of those items. The bar of soap stayed, as well as a change of clothes.

Buster came over and nosed Dillon's arm. "Well, boy," Dillon said. "I've got a long trip to go on. Cassie needs me."

Recognizing Cassie's name, Buster cocked his head and perked up his ears.

"Thatta boy. We'll find her."

Throughout the next couple of hours Dillon packed some canned goods and freeze dried meals in his bugout bag. It wasn't anything to write home about, but in a pinch—and this certainly qualified as a pinch—he wouldn't starve.

He checked on Holly several times making sure she was okay, but after what they had just done, it was more than obvious she was okay. And men were supposed to fall asleep after a good...what should he call it? A good...? He couldn't even say it because it would disrespect a woman of Holly's caliber. Dillon wasn't one to slam-bam-thank-you-ma'am, especially a colleague he admired. He guessed Holly would probably give him the cold shoulder in the morning and that was something he was not looking forward to.

Moving around and burning off some of his nervous energy made him feel better, in fact, sleepy so if he was going to get an early start in the morning, he'd better get some shut eye.

The problem with Buster still worried him. The dog

had become accustomed to city living in an environmentally controlled environment, otherwise known as central heat and air. Maybe he'd let Holly stay here until he got back, which he figured would be about two weeks.

There, that was it. She'd have Buster as company and the loud bark would scare off any intruders. He also wouldn't have to worry about any hurt feelings or awkward morning-after greetings, not after what they had shared. Wow! What the fuck was wrong with him? Bedding the opposing attorney. Now that would definitely be against some ABA rule that could lead to a disbarment, but at the moment, he couldn't think what it would be.

Dillon went to his bedroom, Buster close behind. He stood at the door wondering if he should get in bed with her and go back to sleep. It was like he was invading her personal space. Yeah right, after they had grinded and practically broken the bed, laughing at it afterwards. Oh what the hell? He slid back into bed next to Holly and pulled the sheet up over his chest.

Buster trotted over to his dog bed, spun around a few times, then pillowed into it. Dillon's thoughts soon took him to the logistics of getting out of town: which roads to take, amount of water to bring, so many things to go over, and as he thought about crossing the Atchafalaya Basin, he drifted off to sleep.

When morning came, Dillon woke with a start. It was the coffee that he smelled first. Maybe the electricity had come back on during the night. Maybe he had been all wrong about the EMP. Maybe last night didn't happen.

He swung his legs off the bed and went to the kitchen to find Holly sitting at the table, sipping coffee.

"Want a cup?" Holly asked, as if nothing had happened.

"Yes," Dillon replied, running his hands through his morning hair.

Using her uninjured arm, Holly poured him a cup of coffee from a metal pan.

"How did you make this?"

"While you were sleeping I found a bag of charcoal and matches and started a fire in the grill."

Dillon gave Holly a perplexed look.

"To boil water to make coffee."

"Oh, for a moment I thought the electricity had come back on." Dillon took a sip of coffee. "I'm impressed. I didn't know a city gal knew how to make camp coffee. Putting ground up coffee in the water and then letting the coffee settle to the bottom is something only seasoned campers know about. I didn't know you liked to camp."

Holly smiled. "You never asked," she said, making direct eye contact with Dillon.

Dillon turned away. For some reason, he had no problem staring her down in the courtroom, but here, after their intimate romp, he couldn't think of anything to say other than, "Maybe we need to talk about last night?"

"About what?"

"Like what we did."

Holly made a face. "It still hurts a little. Do you want to look at it."

"What?" Dillon asked. He put the mug down on the table.

"My arm. It still hurts. Do you want to look at it?"

Hmm, well, if she wanted to act like nothing had happened, he'd go along with it.

"Sure. Let me wash my hands first." Dillon got up from the table. "Is the water still working?"

"Pressure's not too good."

"Better than none at all," Dillon said as he turned on

the faucet, wetting his hands. He washed his hands thoroughly, working up a good lather from the pumper soap. He took his time, making sure his fingernails were clean, then washed the back of his hands and up past his wrists. Holding his hands up like a surgeon, he rinsed them under the water for a long time, then repeated the procedure.

Holly watched him, thinking it was overkill until she remembered he had been trained as a medic.

"Can you get me a couple of clean hand towels, hydrogen peroxide, and cotton balls from the bathroom?" Dillon asked. "Check the shelves opposite the mirror."

Holly nodded, walking away.

A knock at the front door sounded, and before Dillon could open his mouth and tell Holly not to open the door, she had already swung the door open. As usual, Buster sauntered up to the door, eager to check out the company. He stood by Holly's side, tail wagging.

Dillon stayed in the kitchen, out of sight of the front door. He was pressed up against the wall and his hand automatically reached for his Glock. *Shit.* He forgot to put it on. His gaze darted around the kitchen, remembering he kept an extra Glock in a hollowed out cookbook. He grabbed it and checked to make sure it was loaded.

Holly opened the door. "Can I help you?"

The disheveled woman standing on the porch didn't say anything. Instead, she pivoted to the side. An expression which Holly didn't understand crept across the woman's face. Holly felt immediate empathy for the woman, and—

A man jumped out of the bushes and in two long strides he rushed the porch and barreled through the door.

Buster started barking rapidly, throaty and low. The man flashed a knife and pushed Holly to the side.

"You do as I say and nobody gets hurt."

The words were met by a more impressive male voice. "*You* do as *I* say and *you* get to *live*."

Chapter 17

Dillon appeared in the hallway, holding his Glock with the barrel pointed directly at the man.

At the sight of his owner, Buster's bravado appeared also and he took a step toward the intruder, growling ominously.

"Get back, Holly," Dillon ordered.

Holly's eyes drifted from the intruder to Dillon as she slowly backed away.

The intruder stood frozen, his eyes glassy, his clothes unkempt and stained. He looked like he hadn't shaved or bathed in days.

"If you want to live, drop your knife and leave," Dillon ordered. "If you come back, all you'll get is a chest full of brass." When the intruder didn't say or do anything, Dillon yelled, "Now!"

The knife clanged to the floor and the guy abruptly turned and ran out the door.

Dillon went to the door and watched the man run down the street, the woman following behind.

"What was that about?" Holly asked. She walked up to Dillon and stood next to him. She craned her head looking at the street, trying to see.

"Didn't your mother ever tell you not to open the door to strangers?"

"Well, yes, but since you were here I—"

"You thought you were safe."

"Yes," Holly's eyes darted from Dillon to the floor then back up to Dillon.

"You weren't." Dillon's tone was gruff. "This is exactly what I meant when I said society as we know it has ended. It's only day one after the EMP and these people can sniff out weakness faster than a hound dog can sniff out a fox. They will do whatever they can to take what is ours. You can never let your guard down. Ever. Do you understand?"

Holly nodded.

"And as far as you are concerned," Dillon admonished, aiming his attention at Buster, "that was lame. Some guard dog you are. Waiting until you knew I was here *then* you started acting brave. Big help you were!"

Buster lowered his head, his ears flopping down on his face. He slunk behind the sofa, sensing his owner's dissatisfaction.

"Excitement is over. Let me take a look at your arm," Dillon said.

Sitting at the kitchen table, Dillon untied the bandage on Holly's arm he had carefully wrapped the day before. Holding it by an edge, he tossed it in the garbage. He gently pressed the skin around the ugly-looking cut and checked for any red streaks indicating infection. He debated whether or not to suture it.

"Do you want me to put a couple of stiches in it?" Dillon asked.

"I don't know."

"It will heal faster if I do."

"Will it hurt?"

"You'll feel a little pinch. I'll be gentle, I promise." Using hydrogen peroxide, Dillon sterilized the cut and also the sewing needle and thread. Getting ready, he told Holly to turn her head and look the other way. "Pretend you're a pioneer woman," Dillon said.

"I'd rather not. I like the comforts of the 21st century."

Dillon began the delicate task, but he might as well have been sticking a needle through leather. Her porcelain skin had the texture of hide.

Holly winced each time the needle pricked her skin and when Dillon brought up the string, she could feel it threading through her.

"You finished yet?" Holly asked through clenched teeth.

"One more suture and you're good to go," Dillon said. He snipped the thread and tied it off. "Want to see my masterpiece?"

Holly turned her head and took a quick glance at her throbbing arm. It looked like it had been through a meat grinder. Dried blood stuck to the wispy hairs covering her black and blue swollen arm.

"Pink?" Holly said incredulously. "You used pink thread?" The pink thread Dillon used stood out like a prima ballerina in a wrestling ring.

"Yeah," Dillon said. "What's wrong with pink? I thought you'd like it."

"I guess nothing. I was expecting black or something."

"I was all out of camo thread," he deadpanned. He got up from the table, went to the sink, and disinfected the needle. "Keep it clean, change the bandage every day, and in ten days you can take out the sutures."

"What? Me? Why? Where are you going?"

"In about thirty minutes, I'm heading to New Orleans to find my daughter. I'll be gone a while."

"Using what as transportation?"

"A mountain bike," Dillon said. "I bought two right before Amy died. One for me and one for her. This will be the first time I've used them."

Holly wasn't exactly sure what she was supposed to say to that. *I'm sorry* didn't sound sufficient, and it wasn't like Dillon was fishing for sympathy. It was more of a matter-of-fact statement, so Holly decided not to say anything about it. Instead, she said, "And what am I supposed to do?"

"Stay here and take care of Buster."

"I will not." Holly pushed back from the chair and stood up, indignant at the thought of being a dog sitter.

"It's the best alternative for you *and* Buster. I've already thought it through. I can't take Buster, you can't walk to your house in the burbs, so the best thing for you to do is to stay here. There's food and water, plus Larry and Louise are right next door if you need anything."

"I don't know Larry and Louise."

"Larry knows you. He helped me get you in the house last night."

Holly thought about that a moment. "I'm still not staying."

"Have a plan B?"

"As a matter of fact I do. I'll come with you."

The look on Dillon's face said it all. That was one scenario he hadn't planned on. She'd slow him down, and riding a bike for hundreds of miles wasn't for the faint of heart or one who was out of shape. Dillon wasn't sure the last time Holly had ever done any manual labor or saw the inside of a gym, not that she was out of shape. She was more runway model worthy, what with her being tall and slender. He wasn't sure she could even shoot a gun without dropping it, or be able to handle the recoil. He decided the best course of action was the take the high road and not point out her lack of arm strength.

"You can't," Dillon finally said. "Your body has been

through a tremendous ordeal. When I carried you here yesterday..."

Holly gave him an odd look.

"That's right, I carried you here all the way from the courthouse. You were unconscious the entire time."

"Oh, I didn't realize. Uh, thank you," she said.

"You're welcome." Dillon took a step closer to Holly. "You need to rest and let your body heal."

"I feel fine. I'll ride with you, and I won't slow you down."

"I don't think you're up to a 300 mile bike ride."

"Who said anything about using a bike the whole way?"

Now *that* piqued Dillon's interest.

Chris Pike

Chapter 18

At daybreak, Ryan, Cassie, and James woke to a humid sea breeze. A white egret flew overhead, flapping wings on a silent updraft. Several buzzards circled what was left of the disintegrated plane, while more took up residence in a lone tree battered by shrapnel from the crash.

"We should have seen planes by now," James said.

"I know," Ryan replied. "Something odd must be going on because I haven't seen any jet trails in the sky."

The three survivors shared a meager breakfast of a granola bar and a pack of peanuts, washing it down with a can of Coke. Cassie said she was saving her other food and water for the trip.

Ryan instructed James and Cassie to rummage through the remains of the plane and look for anything that might be useful.

"Like what?" James asked.

"Water, a jacket, food. Hats, especially hats." Ryan squinted at the morning sun. "It looks like it's going to be a scorcher today. Check any backpacks or briefcases you find. I've already looted what was left of the galley.

If you find any water bottles, regardless if it has been opened, take it. And don't throw it away after the water is gone."

"Why?" James asked.

"If we run out of water, we can fill it with whatever water we find, set it in the sun, and let the sun's rays disinfect it," Ryan explained.

"Never heard of that," James said.

"It works."

After gathering what they could, Cassie hoisted her backpack over her shoulders. She had packed the blanket she had slept in, found a hat, an extra shirt, and shoes that didn't match, which didn't matter because fashion really wasn't a worry of hers right now.

Ryan still had on a good pair of hiking boots, a pair of jeans he'd had on for several days, a shirt, and a thin jacket. James was in his business suit, white shirt, and black Oxford lace-up shoes. Not exactly good for hiking. On the other hand, he hadn't planned on any hiking. At least he was in fairly good shape. His wife had seen to it that after his heart attack two years previous, he lost the weight the doctor said to, kept to his diet, and exercised daily. As of the moment, he was glad his wife had nagged him into adopting better habits.

Ryan stepped out of the plane and took a glance around. From the position of the morning sun he surmised they needed to walk in a northerly direction where I-10 should be. Running east to west, the busily traveled interstate should have other roads feeding into it. He vaguely remembered the southern part of Louisiana being dotted with farmland of sugarcane and cotton, so it shouldn't take too long before they came to a farmhouse or a fish camp. There, they could call the authorities to let them know they had survived.

"Come on," Ryan said. "Let's go before it gets too hot. I want to make it to shade before noon.

The three weary travelers set out, unsure how long it would take to find civilization or another friendly face they could trust. As they walked single file, their thoughts on their loved ones, they had no idea the shit storm they were about to walk into. The life they knew, the conveniences of a modern life which kept them comfortable, gave them information at the touch of a button, transported them in an air-conditioned car while listening to their favorite radio station, which drove them away from the crash site, would only be a distant memory soon.

The world they were entering was an unexpected world, one that would test their strengths and would require them to make difficult, life-altering decisions. Alliances would be made, friends lost, and the answers to their innermost questions would be found.

Chapter 19

"What are you talking about?" Dillon asked.

"I own a ranch about a hundred and fifty miles from here, and," Holly said, pausing for emphasis, "we've got horses. You could take a horse the rest of the way to New Orleans."

Dillon only had to ponder that about a short second before he asked, "Where is your ranch?"

"Near the city of Hemphill, Sabine County. It's not too far from the Louisiana border. By car, it's a short drive. Maybe ninety minutes. By bike, I don't know. Maybe a couple of days."

Dillon pondered how long a ninety minute car ride would be. "I'm guessing it would be about as long as the MS 150. Ever done that?"

"Race for the Cure."

"No. I think I'll rename it to Race for the Living." Dillon swung around. "We still have the problem of Buster." He put a hand to his head, thinking. "If he came with us do you think—"

"I'd be happy to look after him at the ranch."

"Thanks. One problem solved about a hundred more

to go. What about food at your ranch?"

"The normal stuff that doesn't go bad. Canned goods, flour, spices, pasta. I got some peaches and tomatoes some neighbors canned for me. Those are still good. There are pecan trees too, and in a couple of months the pecans will be ripe."

"That's good to know. What about water?"

"We have a couple of wells. One is really old that was dug a long time ago. The other one uses an electric pump."

"Hmm." Dillon scratched the stubble on his chin. "The electric one won't do us any good. Does the old one still have water in it?"

"Actually it does."

"What about a windmill to pump the water, and a storage tank?"

"Those haven't been used in years. You won't believe this but the old well is inside the house."

"No shit!" Dillon exclaimed. "Inside the house?" Flabbergasted wouldn't do justice to his thought. "What's a well doing inside your house?"

"When my parents bought the place the only logical place to build a house was where the old farmhouse was. The only problem was that the well was where they wanted to extend the house. After consulting with an architect, they decided to incorporate the well into the add-on.

"Actually, it's quite beautiful and serene. It's in the sitting area that links the old house to the add-on. My dad put a Plexiglas cover on it because he didn't want the cat falling into it, or a mouse, because that would foul the water."

"Good idea," Dillon said, "not to mention the cat wouldn't like to be in there either."

Holly laughed. "You can look through the Plexiglas and see the water at the bottom."

"That's impressive," Dillon commented. "Does it still have a bucket and pulley system?"

"No."

"It doesn't matter. I can rig something up. What about the water quality?"

"As far as I know, it's still good. My dad had an inspector test the water. He said it was better than the local city water."

"Excellent," Dillon said. "We need to get you packed for a two day bike trip." He studied what she had on. "And I think you need to change out of my shirt."

Dillon's gaze dropped to Holly's upper thighs where his button down shirt she was wearing came to. A woman wearing a man's button down shirt that barely covered her ass was the sexiest thing known to man.

"What do you suggest?" Holly asked. "My pant suit is beyond repair."

Dillon couldn't agree more, especially since he had ripped it off. "You're about the same size as my wife was. You can wear something of hers."

"I don't know. I wouldn't feel right wearing something of hers," Holly said.

"If you had known her, you wouldn't be worrying about that. She was a down-to-Earth type of person. You would have liked her."

"I'm sure I would have. You must have had a good marriage."

Dillon nodded. "Don't worry, there's a bunch of stuff that still has the tags on. She was a thrifty shopper. Check the closet in the master bedroom. Wash up or whatever you need to do and pack a bag of clothes. If you need anything personal take that. I'll pack a bigger bag for you. We leave in an hour."

While Dillon rushed around the house packing a bag for Holly, Buster mirrored every step Dillon took, sensing the excitement in the air. Dillon's routine was well known to Buster since Dillon never deviated from the daily routine: the alarm trilled at 5:30 a.m., next was the shower, coffee, breakfast, then out the door by 6:30. Buster spent his days lazing around the house and when he got bored he wiggled through the doggie door leading to the backyard, and if the weather was good he'd find a sunny spot for more loafing.

Squirrels were a problem, and every once in a while if the squirrel wasn't paying any attention, Buster stealthily crawled closer and *bam!* The squirrel would be dispatched.

Holding the limp squirrel in his mouth, some long-forgotten instinct guided Buster to his next action which was to bury the squirrel, caching it for later consumption.

It never quite worked out that way, because whenever Dillon found the squirrel, the loud shouts and hand waving meant discord between Buster and Dillon. Buster normally retreated into the house, confused as to what he had done wrong. It never lasted long, so by the next day, whatever transgression Buster had been guilty of was forgotten.

Holly took a five minute shower, and though the water was cold and the pressure low it felt good to wash off all the grime and sweat. Standing in the shower, naked, she thought back to the previous night. She had admired Dillon from afar for a long time, watching him in the courtroom, the way he carried himself, but she knew he was off limits, being a married man and all. After his wife died, she couldn't bring herself to flirt with him or ask him out for a friendly cup of coffee. While she had hoped he would make the first move, she hadn't expected for them to see who could get his zipper down first.

With her hair wet and a towel wrapped around her body, Holly went to the walk-in closet and perused the clothes belonging to Dillon's late wife. Going through someone else's things felt like trespassing, and as Holly looked through the clothes, she imagined the life they had lived.

There were the standard business clothes consisting of blazers and black pants. Scarves were hung neatly on wooden pegs, organized by color. There were several dresses, perhaps to wear to a nice restaurant. In the custom made closet, Holly opened the drawers and found the exercise wear she was looking for. Going through it, she decided to change into a pair of yoga pants and a matching top, layering a T-shirt over it. As luck would have it, the size 8 tennis shoes were a fit too.

She found a workout jacket and tied that around her waist. If she got cold, she could wear it. Once she got to the ranch, she'd change into something of her own. She always left clothes there so she wouldn't have to spend much time deciding what to take when she visited, which hadn't been much lately.

After her parents died, going back never seemed the same. The house was cold, barren of life.

Times were changing, and she'd probably better get used to the idea of living at the ranch if what Dillon said was true. It couldn't possibly be true, could it? Yet by the way Dillon talked about the EMP and everything he had said from the stalled cars to the lack of water pressure, it made sense.

Holly searched for an extra change of socks and undies, opening bottom drawers, and when she opened the top drawer, she hesitated when she noticed a jewelry box tucked in the back.

She looked over her shoulder. It was quiet and the morning sun streamed through the bedroom windows. Holly listened to Dillon rummaging around the house.

She stared at the jewelry box for a few long seconds, wondering whether or not to open it. Curiosity got the best of her and she reached over and opened it. There were the usual costume jewelry of bangles and necklaces, plus several pairs of earrings. Holly thought Dillon's wife had excellent taste, or maybe it was Dillon with the good taste. Normally a husband bought his wife jewelry. A small wooden box tucked away in the corner caught Holly's attention. Opening it, she saw a gold necklace with an opal pendant and matching earrings.

For some reason, and it was like a force took over her, she tried on the necklace. Even in the low light, the opal shined iridescent colors of the rainbow. Holly's hand went to the necklace and she thought it surely must have been a present from Dillon.

Dillon barreled into the room. "Holly? Are you ready?"

Holly quickly stuffed the necklace under her t-shirt before turning around. Wide-eyed, she said, "Yes, I'm ready."

"Time to go." Dillon tossed her a backpack, and Holly caught it deftly. "Put the plastic bag in there and let's go."

"This is heavier than I thought it would be," Holly said, testing the weight of the backpack.

"There's still time to back out if you want to. The trip won't be easy," Dillon said. "You'll have to keep up, and if you can't I'll have to leave you behind. I have to find my daughter. She's the only family I have left."

Holly slung the pack on her back and looped her arms through the straps. The weight made her stoop over. "What's in it?"

"Dog food."

Holly gave Dillon one of those stares that sends chills through grown men. Dillon recognized it, but didn't waver. That look might work in the courtroom, but Holly was on his home turf now.

"You're making me carry dog food?"

"That's right. There's still time to change your mind because now's the time, not when we get halfway down the road."

Letting out a long held sigh, she said, "I'm good."

"Let's roll then," Dillon said.

Chris Pike

Chapter 20

Dillon decided the best route to Holly's ranch was to take Interstate 10 until it met Highway 90, then head northeast along the rarely travelled back roads until they came to it. It was a practical and safe route because Interstate 10 was known to be the highway of choice to traffic drugs and other contraband, which in turn attracted unsavory characters.

Unfortunately, the quickest way to the smaller highway was by using Interstate 10 for about thirty miles.

All sorts of makes and models of cars and trucks, 18-wheelers, and delivery trucks dotted the interstate.

They passed desperate people who flagged them down, and Dillon had to ignore their cries for help. Only a few would survive, and he couldn't waste any energy on the expendables.

They were the living dead; they just didn't know it yet.

The bike ride to Holly's ranch was anything but easy. Take an injured woman and an out-of-shape dog, and Dillon was forced to stop every hour, letting everybody catch their breath.

When noon rolled around Holly had lagged further and further behind, along with Buster, who was panting heavily. Dillon decided it would be a good time to stop, eat a quick lunch, and take care of necessities before hitting the road again.

"Hey!" Holly yelled, skidding her bike to a stop. "Why are we stopping here? There's a rest stop ahead about five more miles. We can use the restroom and fill up our water bottles."

"There'll be too many people and I don't want to take any chances. You saw what happened at the house this morning. By now, people will be getting more desperate and if they see us with our bikes and gear, it could get real ugly real quick."

"We have to pass by it anyway. I'll be careful."

"No," Dillon said firmly. "And that's final."

"You're armed. Won't that gun you have slung across your shoulder scare people?"

"That gun is an AK."

She gave him an indignant look. "So?"

Dillon swung his leg over the seat, pushed his bike to the side of a tree, and leaned it there. "If I'm rushed, I might only get a few people. You'll be swarmed, and when people have the strength and courage of a crowd, they do all sorts of things." Dillon looked at Holly directly. "Not nice things, if you get my drift, and I don't plan to give anybody the upper hand." Holly acquiesced.

Standing in the shade, Dillon gulped water and wiped his mouth with the back of his hand. "You thirsty too, boy?" he asked Buster, who thumped his tail as if understanding. Dillon dug around in his pack for the dog's bowl then poured some water for Buster, who greedily lapped it up. Taking out a map, Dillon studied it, tracing a line with his finger.

"We'll be leaving the interstate before we get to the

rest stop, so it's a moot point." He looked pointedly at Holly. "Objection, counselor?"

She dropped her gaze. "No."

"We'll take twenty minutes to eat and then we're outta here on time."

"You don't even have a watch, so how do you know when twenty minutes are up?"

"Why the third degree?" he asked gruffly. "When I say it's time to leave, it's time. Understand?"

Holly didn't answer. She was sitting in the shade, picking at a blade of grass while she cradled her throbbing arm. She gently massaged it, an action that didn't go unnoticed by Dillon. Holly had turned away, unaware that Dillon was studying her. She was taking in the country, trying to get her mind off her arm and the fact maybe she physically wasn't up to this bike ride. She'd never admit it, especially to Dillon. It was too late to turn around, so she'd have to buck up and take it. She drank a few sips of water, praying she wouldn't upchuck. Nausea had set in a couple of hours into the bike ride, and she forced herself to nibble on a peanut butter granola bar and a piece of chocolate.

Her thigh muscles mirrored her throbbing arm.

It was quiet sans the low chirping of a cricket and the wind through the trees. A cardinal sang in a nearby tree, another one answered in a similar melody. They had passed hundreds of abandoned cars and trucks, along with a few drivers steadfast in their resolve to stay with their vehicles. Dillon had said it was foolish because they were wasting valuable time and resources remaining with their cars. Nothing owned was worth losing their lives over.

While on their trek, a distressed man had come running up to Dillon, yelling saying he'd pay a thousand dollars for the bike. Dillon ignored him and rode on telling the man, "I wouldn't sell this for a million dollars."

A group of weary travelers walking toward them garnered Holly's attention. She counted five of them, surmising it was a family. The mother was pushing two kids in a stroller while the oldest one, a son, probably about ten, walked alongside his father.

"Excuse me," the male voice called out.

Dillon put down the map and acknowledged he had heard.

The man came running up to Dillon and Holly. He was sweaty and sunburned, and had an ugly and recent purplish bruise on his cheek. "Do you have any water?" the man pleaded. "My wife and kids are dying of thirst."

Dillon looked at the bedraggled kids, a four and five year old in the stroller, the bigger one standing by his dad. Dillon immediately felt sorry for them, hoping that if his daughter needed help, someone would be kind enough to help her.

"I can spare a couple water bottles, but that's it. I'm sorry."

"Thank you so much."

"I have a bottle I can spare, too," Holly said. She got up and handed one over.

"I'm Brad Slaughter. This is my wife Stephanie."

"Nice to meet you," Dillon said without much conviction. "I'm Dillon, that's Holly."

Holly held out a hand to greet the man.

Brad chugged down half a bottle of water then gave the rest to his oldest son. His wife kept the other two water bottles and instructed the youngest kids to sip slowly and not spill any.

"Do you have any news on what's going on?" Brad asked. "We were driving along the interstate when the car died. I thought the battery had gone dead or something then I saw that all the other cars stop about the same time. None of the phones work either."

"You probably won't believe me even if I tell you."

"What is it?" Brad said. "Tell me."

"I'm guessing an electromagnetic pulse has caused this."

"What's an electro..." Brad trailed off, searching for the right word.

"An EMP for short. It's a nuclear bomb that was detonated high in the atmosphere. Anything electrical like computers, cars, and phones won't be working for a long time. Infrastructure has broken down."

"What do you mean?" Brad asked skeptically.

"Transportation, communications, plumbing, anything that our modern society has relied on is not working and won't for the foreseeable future."

"That's hard to believe. If it's true, then why are some of the cars still working?"

"Like older models?"

"Exactly."

"Vintage cars from the 70s and earlier still work because they don't rely on a computer."

"It's still hard to believe."

"Believe it," Dillon said. "Where do you folks live?"

"West side of Houston."

"Hmm." Dillon took note of that, thinking the family was about ten miles west of his house. "You've got about a two day walk ahead of you." Dillon looked at the weary kids and the wife. "Do you have food to last you a couple of days?"

"We already ate the snacks we had."

"I can spare you a few granola bars, but that's about all."

"Thank you," Brad said. "Do you know where we can get any water?"

Dillon motioned to the west. "About ten miles west of here, there's a local motel about a mile off the interstate. Look for the sign that indicates food and gas. Head north and you'll see the motel on the right. There are vending machines—"

"I don't have any change," Brad said.

"Doesn't matter. Break into it."

Brad glanced at his wife. "That would be stealing."

"In times like these, a man has to do what is right for his family, not what is moral. Think about it."

Brad gave Dillon a puzzled expression.

"We have to go now. Good luck to you folks," Dillon said.

About an hour later Dillon, Holly, and Buster had already turned off the highway to a two-lane country road. Holly peddled to catch up to Dillon.

"Why didn't you tell them to stop at the motel that was closer?"

"Because there'd be too many people there, and whatever resources they would need would probably be gone. Besides, they would probably get hurt or robbed of anything they have. Only the locals know about the motel I told them about, so there is probably still some consumable food there. If they're smart they'll rest and spend the night."

"Do you think they'll make it home?"

"Don't know. Maybe if they can find food and water along the way. It won't be pretty. People will be looking out for themselves and family. Strangers will be on their own."

"Then why did you help them?"

"We're only a day away from supplies. They, on the other hand, are several days away. Plus I felt sorry for the kids. I gave them another day to live. It might be all they need."

"I never pegged you for being altruistic," Holly said.

"Don't count on it again," Dillon said as he put muscle to the bike, taking him further ahead of Holly,

trying to keep his mind off of the previous night. He
didn't look back as he gobbled more ground on the
blacktop.

After thirty minutes of a silent bike ride, Dillon
slowed the pace, waiting for Holly to catch up to him.
"It's my turn to ask questions."

"Go for it."

"Why did you take Cole Cassel as a client?"

Holly didn't answer. She kept her gaze focused
straight ahead.

"He's not exactly the type of client you normally
take," Dillon pressed.

Holly shot him an indignant expression.

"Well? Why *did* you?"

"Because I knew Cole in high school."

Now that wasn't something Dillon had expected to
hear, however, it *would* explain some things. Still, only
knowing somebody in high school wouldn't be a good
enough reason to represent them in a murder trial.

There must be something else, he mused.

Dillon glanced at Holly. Her eyes were downcast and
she seemed a million miles away, staring at the
countryside passing them by.

"That's all?" Dillon asked. "So what if you knew him
in high school? I know a lot of people from high school,
but that's no reason to take anyone as a client."

"We had a baby together."

A bombshell wouldn't aptly describe the revelation,
and if there had been a pin to drop Dillon would have
heard it. He became acutely aware of the silence and the
awkwardness of the situation.

Even Buster picked up on the tenseness of the
situation, and he studied his owner. Buster was used to
Dillon's even breathing. His increasing heart rate and
solemn facial expression worried the dog. Dillon's usual

fluid body movements had turned stiff, as if he was afraid of moving.

Buster glanced at Holly. Her breathing had suddenly become irregular, and Buster detected a burst of unusual tension-laced sweat. He didn't fully understand the events leading up to his new pack acting odd, and his animal instincts guided him to be wary.

Several uncomfortable seconds had transpired of Buster trotting, Holly keeping her gaze on the road, Dillon peddling until finally he said, "Oh."

"The cat's out of the bag so I might as well tell you the rest of the story. I wasn't quite eighteen when it happened. I had planned on going to college, and he was from the wrong side of the tracks."

"I think he's still on the wrong side."

"That really wasn't necessary." Holly gave him a wicked stare and Dillon immediately regretted his remark.

"Sorry," Dillon said. He wiped the sweat off of his brow. "Tell me what happened. I'll keep the rest of my editorial comments to myself."

"It was young love. We were so innocent and full of life, thinking our love would conquer the world. It was our senior year and he was a star football player, and had even gotten a scholarship to a small college."

"Some of the best NFL players come from small colleges."

"Cole had a special quality about him, something that people were drawn to. He was always joking and making people laugh. I loved that about him. When you talked to him it was like you were the most important person in the world. We were going to get married."

"Why didn't you?" Dillon asked.

"He had a dark side I didn't know about. Besides, life and reality intervened in a big way. He came from a bad family. I think he used humor to disguise the problems at home. His father beat his mother and him on a regular basis. Once he got big enough to protect himself, his father stopped beating him. His poor mother took the brunt of the abuse.

"Why didn't his mother leave?"

"Why doesn't any battered woman leave?"

Dillon shrugged.

"It's because they don't know where to go. Their self-esteem has been battered to the point they think they aren't worth anything. So they stay," Holly said.

"What happened to him? The man I prosecuted was nothing like you're describing."

"Our senior year of high school, Cole's mother finally got the courage to leave." Holly snuck a peek at Dillon. "Cole told me she had packed a bag to leave and his father shot her dead."

"It keeps getting better, doesn't it? Did Cole's father get life or the death sentence for that?"

A big breath escaped Holly's lips. "He got a death sentence, that's for sure, but not in the way you think. He took the coward's way out and killed himself with a 12 gauge he stuck in his mouth. Cole came home from school and found him on the front porch sitting in a rocking chair dead with half his skull blown off. He found his mother in the bedroom, still breathing, but there was nothing he could do. She died in his arms."

"That's awful," Dillon said. "I'm starting to understand now."

"Cole was never the same after that. He dropped out of school and became sullen. He even started becoming abusive toward me. I was scared to tell him I was pregnant and I hid it from everyone, including Cole. I was so embarrassed. It's small town America and good girls don't do things like that. I finally told him about the pregnancy because I was beginning to show. Baggy clothes can only work for so long." Holly glanced down at the pavement. "I didn't expect his reaction of accusing me that the baby wasn't his. I was shocked. When I tried to explain to him that he was the only boy I had ever been with, he hit me. He told me he hated me. That was the last time I talked to him."

"That's a lot for a seventeen year old to digest. What did your parents do?"

"When I finally told my parents I was pregnant, it was too late to terminate the pregnancy. They told me that unless I put the baby up for adoption they would disown me because they didn't want anything to do with the baby, saying something about the apple doesn't fall far from the tree."

"There are equal sets of genes to pass down. Didn't your parents consider that?"

Holly shrugged. "It doesn't matter now. I had no way to support myself or afford daycare. My mother said she would not babysit. The only jobs in town were at the drive-in, and I couldn't support me and the baby making minimum wage. I grew up really fast."

"What happened to the baby?"

"My parents arranged for a couple in town to adopt the baby. After the birth, I got to hold my baby for only a moment until the nurses came. I wanted so badly to keep my baby, but it was too late. You can't imagine how hard it is to give up your child. I ached for my child for what seemed like forever. I've regretted my decision all my life."

"I can't even imagine."

"Even after all this time the ache in my heart never leaves. I never saw my baby again, and I wasn't allowed to know the couple's name until the baby turned eighteen."

"It's been more than eighteen years since you had the baby, right?"

"Yes." Holly confirmed.

"I don't understand. There are online registers and open records to search."

"It was a private adoption, and since my parents died in a car crash before the baby turned eighteen, any hope of knowing who the adoptive parents were died along with my parents." Holly stopped talking long enough to take a deep breath.

"I still don't understand," Dillon said. "Regardless of your history with Cole, that's not a reason to take him as your client. You don't owe him anything."

"It is when he called and told me he knew what happened to the baby and if I didn't agree to represent him, he'd kill our child."

"He's a real saint. You could've gone to the police."

"I could have, except he told me he'd tell me our child's name if I won the case."

Chapter 21

Dillon kept the pace steady, figuring they could make it to Holly's ranch by noon the next day. After Holly's soul-baring revelation, it became obvious the revered Holly Hudson was human after all. Dillon actually felt sorry for her, surmising that the trauma she experienced as a teenager was one of the reasons she hadn't ever married. Getting burned like that at a young age had to have impacted her in a way she maybe never recovered from.

A serious case of regrets hit him for what he did the previous night. Surely he hadn't taken advantage of Holly during one of her weakest moments. Had he? When she crushed her body against his, the rest took its natural course.

Dillon now worried about how she was doing. Her complexion had taken on an ashen appearance and she rarely used the arm that had been injured the day before. Whenever he asked to see it, she refused.

Buster, on the other hand, he didn't have to worry about. For a dog used to lounging around the house all day, his stamina was surprising.

Intermittently, Dillon glanced at Holly, worried that the ride was too taxing for her. She was a trouper though, never complaining about cramped muscles or the pace.

He took in the vastness that lay before him, from the bare fields and wind-brushed trees, to livestock oblivious to the changing world. Surprisingly, he felt invigorated. The life he had built using brains instead of brawn had come to an abrupt end, a life he thought he'd probably never go back to. The house he shared with Amy sat barren, devoid of the things that make a house a home, among the soon-to-be dying city. He wondered if he would ever see it again, yet without Amy it was only a dwelling, a place to hang his hat and to sleep.

It hadn't been a home for a long time.

What the future would bring he did not know, and he would live day to day, doing whatever it took to survive, whatever it took to find his daughter. He'd build a life with her, although where, he did not know.

They biked along the two-lane country road winding through the countryside, crossing creeks and passing abandoned vehicles.

A rancher sitting high on a horse checking his livestock acknowledged his and Holly's presence by a friendly dip of the hat. Dillon returned an equal friendly dip then peddled on.

The bike ride afforded Dillon time to think and to formulate a plan to find Cassie. After getting Holly to her ranch, making sure she'd be safe, he'd saddle the best horse and he could be in New Orleans by late the next day.

That is, if all went well.

Chapter 22

It was early morning and Dillon had been awake for a while, listening to a rooster crowing in a nearby pasture. Holly had been out like a light the entire night, and slept through the rooster alarm clock.

Tentative morning light cast aside the night and streamed low through the countryside, awakening the land. Doves cooed and cardinals chirped a morning melody. The caw-caw of a crow joined in, the chorus unusually loud. He'd never hear anything like this in the city, and he wondered why he had stayed in the rat race for so long.

Routine probably, or the fear of change. It didn't matter anymore. If Amy was still living they definitely would have been on their way to something different. With Cassie about to be self-sufficient, it should have been Dillon's and Amy's time, a new chapter in their life.

So much for that.

Stretching out on the ground with his hands clasped behind his head, he stared at the tree above him until the leaves blurred together. His thoughts drifted back to his wife. He missed her terribly. Missed the way her hair fell to her shoulders; the way she laughed at all of his stories, pretending she had never heard them before; the way she greeted him when he came home. He missed everything about her.

He hadn't even taken one thing of hers from their house, and he silently cursed at the stupidity of that. Not even her favorite piece of jewelry. Yet, closing his eyes, he could imagine every detail of her face: the dimples in her cheeks when she laughed, the laugh lines framing her eyes, her sparkly eyes. Regardless how much he thought about his wife, the life they had made together ceased to exist the moment she died. Maybe it was time for him to move on, to start really living again instead of merely existing, because that's what he had been doing for the past two years.

It had taken Dillon a long time to consider himself unmarried, even wearing his wedding ring up until a few months ago.

He had made camp under an oak tree with a splendid canopy. The grass was soft, rocks a minimum, and being in the country had indeed rejuvenated him. Humans weren't meant to sit at a desk, staring at a computer for eight hours a day, and Dillon wasn't any exception. Using his muscles had felt great, though his back and legs were sore, and all the fresh air had reenergized him. He thought the same of Buster. His dog's eyes were brighter and his senses more alert.

He turned toward Holly, now stirring. A gold chain peeked out from under her shirt. He surmised she had worn it to the courthouse that day. Funny that he hadn't noticed it during their carnal romp, then again, he wasn't really looking at jewelry, not when he had his face buried in her breasts. Dillon wasn't much into jewelry, but for some reason he took notice of it now, wishing he had taken something of Amy's from the house. He cursed at the stupidity of not getting anything of his wife's to give to his daughter.

Out of habit he had put his wallet in his back pocket on the way out of the house. Taking it out, he rifled through the useless credit cards, various membership IDs, and insurance cards. He wanted to toss them, yet at the same time it was proof of who he was. If the shit had hit the fan like he thought, although these cards were useless now, they were evidence of his life. He thought it strange how IDs and plastic cards gave validity to a person's life. A few dollar bills and twenties padded his wallet and he was tempted to throw them away because paper money wouldn't be used for a while until a new barter system came into effect.

An egg-laying chicken would be worth more than a bar of gold in the near future. Still, he couldn't muster the courage to toss the cards.

Tucked away in the wallet was his favorite picture of Cassie and Amy. Hesitant to take it out, he glanced at Holly, making sure she was still sleeping. He didn't want her to know his private pain. Holding the picture in his hand, a wave of sadness overcame him, and he was acutely aware of how empty he felt without his family. His wife had been his partner and equal. Together, they were whole.

The picture had been taken at their favorite steak restaurant on her fortieth birthday. Cassie was smiling. A piece of birthday cake with a sparkly candle illuminated Amy's smiling face. An opal locket hung on her décolletage. It had been her birthday present, something she'd planned to give their daughter someday.

He put the picture back in his wallet, and glanced at Holly. Her hair was a tattered mess and her fair complexion had turned pale. He had noticed that she continued to favor her injured left arm, and on the last hour of the ride the previous day, she rode with one hand on the handle bars. It worried him. She shifted positions, turning toward him.

Dillon turned on his side, propping an elbow on the ground. "You don't look so good."

Holly met his eyes for a moment but didn't say anything. Rising from the ground which had been her bed for the night she said, "You sure do know how to make a girl feel pretty."

"That's not what I meant."

"I mean you don't look well."

"Wrong answer. Try again."

"You know what I mean."

Holly stood and massaged her lower back with her good arm. "I'm not used to sleeping on hard ground, that's all. I didn't sleep well. I've got a kink in my back that's been bothering me. As soon as I get a good night's sleep I'll be fine."

"You won't have long to wait for that. In a few hours, you'll be in your ranch home." Dillon rose from his makeshift bed and walked over to Holly. "Let me do that."

"Do what?"

"Massage your back."

Holly started to protest, but Dillon had already had put his hand in the small of her back. To steady her, he placed the palm of his other hand over her décolletage, pressing down. Standing, she rolled with the circular strokes of his warm hand, and felt something stir in her bosom. The strength of his arms was noticeable, and she breathed heavy and slow, trying to control her hammering heart. She'd die if Dillon knew her heart was beating at breakneck speed; if he knew that the reason she didn't sleep well was because she had been thinking about him during the night.

She swallowed audibly.

"How's your arm?" Dillon asked.

"It's good." Holly broke loose from Dillon and turned away. She licked her lips, suddenly aware of her thirst.

"Can I see it?" Dillon asked.

Holly waved him off. She dug around in her backpack, found a water bottle, and took a sip of water. "Let's get going, okay? I'm eager to get to the house, take a bath, and get into a real bed."

"Does your back feel better?" Dillon asked.

"It does. Thank you for that."

"A week ago if I had offered you a backrub, I think you might have called HR on me. Either that or slapped me."

Holly snuck a hesitant peek at Dillon. After a long pause she finally said, "I think you got your answer the other night."

"I thought maybe you had forgotten."

"It was a moment of weakness, that's all. I'm sorry. It won't happen again."

"I was hoping it would," Dillon said. He moved closer to her, challenging her personal space.

Holly shot him an indignant look. "Well it won't, so forget about it."

How could he forget about it? Holly had practically ripped his shirt off while he carried her to the bedroom. How could he forget the way she arched her back when he touched her? Or the way she nibbled on his ear afterwards?

"Yeah," Dillon said gruffly. "Forget about it."

Holly had turned away and bit her lip. She felt something akin to static electricity being generated between them, and if he touched her again, she might not be able to resist. His presence was commanding, and though she wouldn't admit to it, if Dillon had run for District Attorney like the rumor mill had it, she would have voted for him, courtroom adversary or not. His ethics were impressive and his drive for justice couldn't be dismissed. Holly admired him for that, although what had happened scared her. She had lived her life one way for so long, and now Dillon had challenged her world. She was rethinking her single life, especially after the way Dillon treated her. She had never met anyone like him. A complicated man. Strong when it mattered, gentle where it counted.

Dillon grabbed her arm and turned her around. "It meant something to me. I want you to know that."

As she held his intense gaze, for the first time she noted the color of his eyes. Brown, though that wouldn't aptly describe the intensity of his gaze, and the longer they looked at each other, the more uncomfortable she became. She was the first to turn away.

"It's only us now, out here, in the middle of Nowheresville, USA," Dillon said. "There aren't any clients to impress or juries to sway. No legal posturing. It's okay for us to lean on each other, to need each other, to help each other out. I give a damn good massage, so anytime you want one, all you have to do is ask."

"I'll keep that in mind." Holly knelt and struggled to roll the sleeping bag. Her bad arm hurt with every movement.

"I'll do that."

"You've already done enough. I can manage."

"I wasn't asking." Dillon stepped in, whisked the sleeping bag away, and deftly tucked it into a tight roll.

"Thank you," Holly said.

"You're welcome." Dillon tied off the string and handed the bag to Holly. "I'm sure your turn will come to help me out someday."

Truer words couldn't have been spoken.

Chapter 23

It was quiet for a while as Dillon and Holly went about the business of breaking camp. Buster greedily ate his breakfast and slurped a bowl of water. He silently excused himself to a patch of grass where he did his business. Dillon poured a few drops of water on what remained of the smoldering fire then scraped dirt over it, making sure no embers were left.

"I've been meaning to ask you who's been taking care of the horses at your ranch."

Holly knelt and retrieved her backpack, and with a heave she slung it over her back. "The ranch foreman, Hector Hernandez. My parents hired him a long time ago. He's trustworthy and keeps the place up. I pay him from royalty generated from an oil well drilled several years ago."

"Hmm. I guess the rumor mill was right."

"About what?" Holly asked.

"About your land sitting on what could be the next Spindletop."

Holly laughed. "That's what people talk about? Thinking my land is sitting on some gigantic oil field?"

She shook her head. "Spindletop, the gusher that started the oil industry in Texas. It wasn't far from here, you know?"

"I know. Near Beaumont."

"Believe me, if the well drilled on our place produced a fraction of what Spindletop did, do you think I'd be playing nursemaid to a bunch of greedy corporations and murderers?"

"It makes you a lot of money."

"Money doesn't make you happy," Holly said.

"What would make you happy?"

Holly thought about that a moment because the question was a little too personal. She had become used to hiding behind an invisible wall, a fortress surrounding her personal space that had a neon sign flashing loud and clear: Don't get too close.

Dillon was too dense to notice it. Or maybe he did and was surreptitiously chipping away at it as if he was a master carver and Holly was a wooden block. Then again, perhaps he was blind and didn't see the neon lights flashing.

Here she was, forty-something, never married, never been to a PTA meeting, baked cookies for a soccer team, made homecoming mums, been to a swim meet, or debate competition. She had missed out on so much life because of that damned wall.

Well, shit.

Holly looked at him for a thoughtful second. "If you had asked me a week ago, I would have said winning a case makes me happy. Shopping at Nordstrom's or eating lunch at a nice restaurant would have made me happy. Now? After all that's happened, I don't know. Maybe I'd be on my ranch with my husband and kids. We'd have a couple of dogs. It would be a working ranch with cows, and maybe some crops. I'd get involved with the county rodeo. Maybe even tinker in breeding. There's money in that.

"I'd grow a garden and have fruit and nut trees. I'd live a simpler life, away from the big city, and the noise and the pollution. Maybe the EMP is what I needed to kick me in the butt so that I could reassess my life. As of now, I'm not sure when and if this EMP problem ever goes away that I'd move back to the city."

"You and I are in agreement on that."

"How so?" Holly asked.

"Amy and I had decided to move out of Houston to someplace where we would have purchased a tract of land."

"You still could."

"I suppose so," Dillon said. "The dream life wouldn't be the same without someone to share it with."

"It wouldn't."

The personal revelations and amount they had in common made Dillon feel uncomfortable now. He was getting to know Holly more than he anticipated. He had planned to get her to her ranch, make sure she had something to eat, was safe, then the next day he'd be on his way, probably never seeing her again. He hadn't planned on caring.

"Getting back to the problem at hand. What exactly does Hector do?"

"Looks after the house. Makes repairs, paints, mows the grass, looks after the livestock. There isn't much livestock left, only a few cows and the horses. Maybe some chickens if the bobcats haven't gotten them all."

"Egg layers?"

"Yes."

"Good. I'll make you scrambled eggs for breakfast tomorrow. I could use a hot meal."

"You're a man of many talents."

"I have many talents you don't know about," Dillon said with a wink.

Holly smiled demurely.

"Got any goats?"

"No. Why?"

"Fresh cabrito makes a fine meal."

Holly laughed. "In that case, I wish we did have some!"

"It's good to hear you laugh," Dillon said.

When he met her eyes, Dillon thought he saw a flickering of something he didn't know the venerable Holly Hudson was capable of. Maybe it was admiration for a fellow colleague even if they had been on the opposite sides of the courtroom. Maybe it was the fact she was tired and her reflexes were sluggish. Whatever it was, he was starting to like it.

He quickly cleaned the makeshift camp, making sure they didn't leave any trash behind. While he worked he ate another granola bar, along with a can of sardines which packed a good punch of protein. He washed his breakfast down with half bottle of water. Buster had already eaten his morning share and done his business, which Dillon covered with dirt and branches.

Holly had already packed and was straddling the bike. "I'm ready to go when you are."

Several hours later after a silent bike ride on blacktop roads, they turned onto a caliche road heading to the entrance of Holly's ranch. It was a good thing Dillon hadn't tried to find this by himself because it was definitely off the beaten path. A half hour of peddling on the bumpy road left the ragged crew of three covered with a thin layer of white dust. It stuck to their arms, hair, backpacks, clogged their nostrils, and when Dillon checked on Buster, he was suffering too.

Coming to the entrance, Dillon stopped and took out a bowl from his pack, poured water in it, and gave it to Buster. After his thirst was satiated, Buster found a soft spot in the weeds and sat down on his haunches, panting. Their two day bike ride had finally come to an end.

It was noon and the sun shone in the brilliant October sky. A lone buzzard floated on a silent updraft, while a breath of wind rustled the trees.

Dillon took a sip of water and let his eyes roam over the property. Several types of oaks, towering pines, and uncleared brush lined each side of the winding caliche road leading to Holly's house, which was partially hidden by the thick canopy of trees.

Without the steady hum of spinning tires upon rock, it was quiet. Only the sounds of the country filled the air. The chirping of a field sparrow broke the silence, followed by more. A flock of redwing blackbirds flew overhead. A breath of wind rustled the tall grass.

"It looks like Hector has been falling down on the job judging from how high the grass is," Dillon said.

"Maybe the mower isn't working," Holly replied.

Dillon and Holly had stopped at the metal gate where a chain with thick links was looped through the gate. It was secured with a heavy lock.

"You always lock the place, even way out here?" Dillon asked.

Holly rubbed her eyes and splashed water on her face. "It shouldn't be locked because it's too much trouble to unlock it every time. It only *looks* locked. Thieves are opportunists and if they see a lock while driving by, they don't bother."

"Makes sense," Dillon said. "I'll do the honors and open it. I don't want you to hurt your arm any more than it already is."

"My arm *is* bothering me," Holly acknowledged. She gingerly touched the bandage covering her arm.

"I'll take a look at that when we get inside." When Holly was about to protest, Dillon cut her off, his tone firm. "It's not a question this time. I need to look at it."

"If you insist."

Dillon dropped his bike's kickstand then made sure his bike was stationary. He went to the gate and bent over to undo the chain. "This is odd," he said.

"What is?" Holly asked.

"I thought you said the gate wasn't locked."

"It shouldn't be. Hector never locks the gate. Let me try it." Going over to the gate, she tugged on the lock using her good arm.

"What'dya know. It *is* locked. That's really strange." Holly tried to straighten her injured arm and when she did she let out a grunt of pain.

"I'll do that," Dillon said. "What's the combo?"

"1600. As in 1600 Pennsylvania Avenue. It's hard to forget. Can you imagine what Washington must be like now?"

"They never get anything useful done anyway," Dillon said. "Good riddance to all of them."

Holly was taken aback by that. "We still need government."

Dillon patted his AK slung over his shoulder. "This is all the government I need."

"Oh really? You some kind of anti-government guy?"

"I'm a practical guy. Government has nothing to do with it. Like I told you," he said pointedly, moving closer to her, crossing that personal threshold again, and taking ownership of a small bit of it, "we're on our own. Seen any government vehicles? Police cars? Or anybody in uniform for that matter?"

Holly, acutely aware of how close he was, held her ground, and said nothing.

"They are helping their families. I'm the only one going to be able to help mine."

Dillon fiddled with the dial until the shackle popped open. Unwrapping the chain, he pushed open the gate only wide enough for them to squeeze through, not wanting to call attention any more than he had to. He motioned for Holly to go through and as she was about to peddle in, Buster popped in front of her. He loped through in three long strides, sniffing the ground as he went.

"I guess your dog doesn't know about ladies first."

"He only speaks dog," Dillon said, still holding open the gate, "and a few words of English, especially when it comes to food."

A smile broke across Holly's face.

When Buster crossed over onto Holly's land, he stopped and lowered his head, letting his eyes roam over the countryside. A strange scent caught his attention. The ruff on his back prickled and he growled low in his throat.

"What's wrong with Buster?" Holly asked. She was straddling her bike with her feet planted on the hard-packed caliche.

"I'm not sure. I've never seen him like this." Dillon went over to his dog. "Buster, you okay, boy?"

Dillon reached down to comfort his dog, and without warning or indication, a bullet whizzed by Dillon a fraction of a second after his brain registered the crack of a rifle shot. The bullet slammed into the tree behind him. Splinters of bark flew like missiles in every direction, and before Dillon could process what had happened, another bullet struck the dirt in front of him.

Chapter 24

"Get down!" Dillon shouted. "Get off your bike!" He fell into the tall grass and belly-crawled to a tree.

Buster took off running into the brush.

Holly scrambled off her bike, letting it fall down. She clambered into the culvert and pressed her body into the grass and weeds.

"Buster. Buster! Come back here!" Holly yelled. She poked her head above the culvert.

"Keep your head down and stay quiet!" Dillon ordered.

She shot him a terrified look then melted into the grass. Her thumping heart beat at breakneck speed. She was yards from any real cover, and lying in the culvert without any real protection made her feel vulnerable. Holly Hudson didn't like being a sitting duck.

Breathless, she said, "I don't want to stay here. There's no protection."

"Stay there."

"No. I'm coming to where you are."

"Damn it, stay there!"

"I'm coming."

"Shit." Holly popped her head above the grass line. "For God's sake get on your stomach, and don't raise your head again. And take your backpack off!" Dillon craned his neck trying to find her. "I think you can wiggle under the barbed wire fence. Use your elbows and toes to come over here. Stay to the natural contours of the ground and keep your butt down. Wouldn't want that nice ass of yours to get shot."

Several bullets whizzed by and smacked into the surrounding trees, splintering the bark.

Kneeling behind the tree, Dillon flinched and waited.

The sound was different than the first volley, lighter, probably a smaller caliber rifle. Dillon speculated there was only one shooter who was changing his weapons trying to fool them into thinking there were two shooters or worse, panic them, hoping they'd run out in the open.

Staying close to the ground, Holly wiggled over to Dillon. Fortunately, they had taken cover behind a centuries old oak tree with a trunk circumference large enough to hide two full grown men.

"Don't you think you need to return fire?" Holly asked.

"Not now. They don't know we are armed, and I want to keep it that way. Besides, we need to always conserve ammo. I doubt any guns shops will be open in town."

Dillon took off his backpack and dug around in it, searching for his Les Baer 1911 Thunder Ranch Special 45 ACP. The 1911 hailed as one of the most successful pistol designs of the 20th century, being fielded in both World Wars. Weighing in at 2.4 pounds sans the 8 round magazine, the 3.5 pound trigger pull combined with excellent sights made this a gun that could turn even a novice into a force to be reckoned with.

Dillon considered the Thunder Ranch Special to be the scalpel of pistols while the Glock was more like a reliable machete. Dillon could make excellent hits at 50 yards with the Glock, but the Thunder Ranch Special could do the same at 100 yards. In situations where accuracy was paramount and the environment lacked desert sand, he would normally choose the Thunder Ranch Special for himself.

The Glock was still Dillon's first pick when he did not know the environment in which he would be operating. Clean or dirty, he knew without doubt that the Glock would still bark when he called on it.

"Here, take this," Dillon said. "You right handed?"

Holly nodded.

He placed the large steel pistol into Holly's right hand. "You'll need this to protect yourself. You know how to use this?"

"I don't like guns."

"Perfect." Dillon's tone couldn't have been any more sarcastic. "It's one of the most reliable guns I have, and now's not the time to get in a debate about guns," he said gruffly. "First rule: Don't point it at anything you don't want to kill. Got that?"

Holly didn't answer.

"Got it?" His tone was gruffer.

"Yes."

"I'm going to give you a quick lesson in how to handle guns, so listen closely. Since you've got small hands, hold it tight like your life depends on it. A limp wrist hold could cause it to jam. Hold it in your right hand like you're trying to impress a big burly client with a firm handshake. Wrap your left hand around the grip until skin is touching all sides of the grip. Push the safety down with your right thumb. Keep your trigger finger straight until you're on target and ready to pull the trigger."

When Dillon took her left hand, she winced in pain at the rough movement. He positioned her hands around the 1911 to his satisfaction, glad that she wasn't fighting him.

"How's that arm holding up?"

"Good enough."

"Since this kicks like a mother, you'll need to lock your wrists when shooting. You'll be able to absorb the recoil better that way since you're not muscled up. If you have to shoot, your adrenaline will probably kick in and you probably won't even feel your hurt arm. Here are a few extra loaded magazines. Keep them ready in your back pocket."

She took the magazines, stuffed them in her pocket, and defiantly looked him straight in the eyes. "I'm stronger than I look."

Holly let out a long breath she had been holding and sat back, Indian-style with her legs crisscrossed. Dillon was on one knee, the AK at an angle. Using the tree as cover, he checked the surrounding countryside for an escape route. While they had good cover, there wasn't another viable tree in the near vicinity to completely hide them. There was a straight line of sight from the house to the tree, and too much brush had been cleared. The small oaks and pines that dotted the land were useless to them.

They were trapped. On the other hand, the shooter might be trapped also.

"What's behind the house?" Dillon asked.

"A garden."

"Any fruit trees?"

"A peach tree, but it's not very big. There's a pump house about fifty yards away."

Dillon thought about that for a moment. The shooter might be able to make a run for it, out the back door, and they'd never know who it was. As long as it was light, they couldn't move.

"Any idea who might be in the house? Anyone who wanted your property?" Dillon asked. While he talked he checked each magazine making sure they were fully loaded.

"I don't know. Maybe." "Maybe who?"

"I don't know. I hate to badmouth anyone."

"Holly!" Dillon said in a low voice, his jaw tight. "We've got someone trying to kill us. Who could be in the house?"

"There's a jerk who owns neighboring property." Holly motioned with her head. "Clyde Higgins, on the other side of the fence line. Ever since he started a brush fire that almost burned down my parents' house, my parents and him didn't get along."

"How'd the fire start?"

"He was stupid enough to burn brush on a windy day in November. The land was dry and the fire got out of control really quickly and it came to within yards of our house. Thankfully, a firetruck got here in time to put out the fire. To top it off, he offered to buy the land after my parents died, even had the gall to draft a contract and give it to me during their funeral."

"He sure didn't waste any time, did he?"

"No, he didn't," Holly said.

"Does he have any military training?"

"Not that I know of."

"Married or kids?"

"Wife left him a few years ago. He's got grown kids but I've never met them. What are you going to do?"

"Make whoever it is in the house leave."

Chapter 25

While Dillon was formulating a plan, what sounded like a slamming screen door got his attention. He tapped Holly on the leg and put his index finger to his lips, swung his AK up, pressed the butt to his shoulder, and flipped the safety down to the fire position.

A 123 grain hollow point was already in the chamber so charging the rifle wasn't necessary. Thirty more rounds waited in the magazine as backup.

He pivoted around the side of the tree, sighting on the front door of the stately house. A wide porch wrapped around the front and sides of the house. There were long windows suitable for taking advantage of cross breezes, and a crawl space under the first floor was camouflaged with white lattice work. A gorgeous country house by any standards. Not all that good from a tactical standpoint with all the windows and doors, but the second story provided an advantage by looking out over the land. It had a 360 degree view.

Dillon rested his finger beside the 4.5 pound trigger, his heart racing from the surge of adrenaline. He preferred the lighter trigger pull over a heavier one because the lighter one didn't jerk the rifle off target on distance shots.

Prior to leaving his house, Dillon had installed an Aimpoint sight on his AK using his bore sighting tool. In the past, he was never more than two inches off at one hundred yards when he checked his bore sighting. Fortunately, the Aimpoint survived the EMP because it was stored in his metal gun safe.

He kept his eye on the Aimpoint's red dot, a piece of equipment that gave him a speed advantage over an opponent without a red dot sight. Sighting a target using one focal point instead of lining up the standard front sight and rear sights shaved off a few tenths of a second. In most gunfights the person who got the first accurate shot off was usually the winner.

He scanned the house and the surrounding acreage looking for movement or another door.

Without taking his eyes away from the sight, Dillon asked, "Is the backyard fenced in?"

"Yes. There's a gate leading to a pasture road, and—"

"Shhh, listen." Dillon lowered his rifle a smidgen and cocked his head in the direction of the sound. "I think it's a car engine turning over."

"I thought you said cars don't work."

"They don't, except for older models."

"They wouldn't be so foolish to drive past us would they?" Holly asked.

"I don't think so. Is there a back way out of here?"

"Yes. The dirt road on the side of the house leads to the back of the property. A gate there takes you to a farm-to-market road that goes in both directions."

"Come on," Dillon said. "Let's go. Stay behind me."

Dillon moved swiftly toward the house, keeping a firm grip on his AK, dodging brush and taking cover where he could find it. He sprinted to one tree then another until he was up to the house. He crouched, taking cover behind the steps leading to the porch.

The sound of tires on gravel echoed in the distance. The wind rustled the leaves and a setting sun cast long shadows on the land.

Holly kept up as best she could and when she came to her house, she looked left and right then ducked in the shade of a leafy overgrown ligustrum.

Keeping his head down, Dillon sprinted to the edge of the house. He leveled his AK and swung around as an old light-colored truck sped in the distance along the dusty road. Flashes of the red taillights glowed through the billowing dust kicked up as the truck fishtailed around a corner, disappearing behind the tree line.

Dillon thought about firing a warning shot until common sense dictated otherwise. He'd save the bullet for when he had a good shot.

Frustrated, he turned to Holly. "Does that Clyde Higgins neighbor own a truck?"

"I haven't seen him in years, so I don't know."

"It must be someone you know or some local because they knew about the back road out of here."

"Some of my parents' old friends, but nobody I know who would try to..." Holly trailed off, the realization sinking in regarding what had happened. "It's only been a few days since the EMP and people are already trying to kill each other."

"I told you it would get bad."

"I can't believe it."

"You just witnessed it. Sit here while I go in and clear the house."

Holly sat on the lowest step on the front porch while Dillon searched the house.

It was quiet.

The lonely hand of the wind touched the trees and grass. Low clouds floated in the waning light, a crow cawed, and buzzards circled the adjoining pasture.

155

Something rustled the bushes adjacent to the house.

Startled, Holly gripped the 1911 semi-automatic and brought it up, pointing it in the direction of the sound. Her heart beat harder and she held the gun tight.

A dark form burst through the bushes and Holly flinched. She remembered what Dillon had said: *Keep your finger off the trigger guard until you're ready to shoot. Then you shoot to kill.*

She really didn't need to go over that. She already knew it.

Old muscle memory took over at that point, and the times her dad had taken her hunting and target practicing paid off now. Rarely advertising her knowledge or skills of firearms, it was best she kept it to herself. Her eyes narrowed and she squeezed shut her right eye, keeping the focus on the front sight. She forgot about her wounded arm.

She'd kill if she had to, regardless who it was, the circumstances, or the reasons. This was her land, and if someone brought the fight to her, she'd give it right back. The bushes came alive.

Holly pressed her index finger to the trigger, ready to dispatch whoever it was.

Buster barreled out of the bushes and relief washed over her. She released the tension in her shoulders, dropping them, lowered the 1911, and whistled for Buster.

The big dog came sauntering up to her, wiggling enthusiastically, tail thumping, blissfully unaware he had been in the crosshairs of her gun. He was panting and droplets of slobber flung off of his tongue.

"Oh my God," Holly said in exasperation. "You scared me half to death. Come here, you big lug."

Buster sidled up to her, wiggling and favoring his right front paw. She took a handful of fur and ran her hands along his back checking for any wounds. His underbelly was muddy and wet, and Holly scrunched her nose at his pungent smell. She felt the pads of his toes and recognized why Buster was limping. After pulling out several stickers, Holly said, "What have you been doing? Chasing a rabbit or something? What are we going to do with you?"

Rummaging around in her backpack, Holly found a water bottle and took a swallow. Buster watched her with an eager eye. Taking his cue, Holly poured water in her hand and encouraged Buster to drink.

Sweat beaded on her forehead, and she put her hand to it. With her adrenaline dump waning, she became aware of her throbbing arm, which kept pace with every heartbeat.

Tentatively, she pulled back the bandage and inspected the wound. The skin around where the shrapnel had sliced her arm looked angry and red, but it wasn't that she was worried about. It was the red streaks slithering up her arm like a deadly anaconda searching for prey.

Chapter 26

"All clear!" Dillon yelled from inside the house. "You can come in now."

Rising from the steps, Holly opened the screen door and walked inside, Buster behind her. She stood in the foyer. The front door was heavy and tended to shut by itself so Holly took an old metal iron and propped it against the door.

The house looked like it always did. Framed pictures decorated the end tables in the formal living room. A watercolor painting from a bygone era hung in the entryway, while other framed pictures decorated the living room and connecting dining room. This front part of the house was rarely used, a throwback to more formal times.

The den area was quite comfortable with a sofa and matching La-Z-Boy recliner. A big screen TV sat upon a credenza, something Holly had bought her parents because they liked to watch TV. Now it would be collecting dust.

"Any sign of Hector?" Holly asked.

"I've got a bad feeling about this," Dillon said. "I'll check the pasture in a few minutes. Did you see the buzzards in the tree?"

"I did."

"They sit there until their meal gets ripe." Dillon cleared his throat. "If you know what I mean."

Holly gasped. "Hector?"

Dillon nodded. "Whoever was here probably killed Hector."

There was a lull in conversation at the somber thought. Dillon and Holly turned their attention to Buster, who was oblivious to the situation. He was sniffing the new dwelling, running his nose all along the floor, taking his time to inspect the house.

"This is your home now, Buster," Holly said, "at least for the time being." She walked over to the recliner, slung her backpack off her shoulder, and slumped in the chair.

Dillon was already in the kitchen perusing the pantry, taking stock of the contents. His backpack was on the kitchen table. "The food is still here, so I don't know what that guy was doing here. Does anything look out of place? Or missing?"

Holly glanced at the corner of the room where screws had been placed in each hardwood plank running parallel to the wall. It didn't appear those had been removed or tampered with. "Don't think so. My parents didn't buy much in the form of valuables. One of their main pastimes was checking their bank and stock accounts, watching their money grow. They were extremely frugal. Not cheap," Holly emphasized, "frugal. There's a difference."

"I'm not sure money or stocks will do us much good anymore," Dillon said. He crunched on a few saltine crackers, followed by a big gulp of water. Buster came up to him wanting a cracker. He thumped his tail. Dillon slipped him a cracker, which Buster inhaled. "Hey, do you mind going back to where the bikes are and bringing them up here? The bugout bags too?"

"Okay." Holly rose and when she did, stars appeared in front of her eyes. Trying to steady herself, she held onto the arm of the recliner. Teetering on wobbly legs, she said, "I think I'm going to..."

Dillon turned as Holly slumped into the plush chair. He rushed over to her.

"Holly! Holly, what's wrong? Can you hear me?" He tapped her cheek.

There was no response. Taking her wrist, he took her pulse. It was weak. Her skin was clammy and had taken on the color of old milk, and a sour odor emanated from her wounded arm. Her face felt hot. He carefully peeled back the bandage, and when he did, he made a face.

"Shit. This is bad." He stared at the red streaks feathering up her arm toward her shoulder. "Blood poisoning," he said quietly.

Out of all the medications he had stocked up on, antibiotics was not one of them. Too bad they didn't have the Russian system of walking into a drugstore and buying antibiotics without a prescription. Doctors were too stingy with those, afraid the overuse would result in strain-resistant germs. Besides, the pharmaceutical industry paid dearly for lobbyists to protect their holdings.

Not anymore, Dillon thought.

The old ways would go the way of the buggy whip, providing new opportunities and a different way of life. Let the lobbyists and the lawmakers who'd created this mess go to Hell.

Dillon retrieved a hand towel from the kitchen, poured a little water on it, folded it, and placed it on Holly's forehead. She needed help cooling down. He opened the windows in the room to let in a cross breeze.

While Holly was passed out, Dillon searched the house for any unused antibiotics. He checked the usual places: bathroom vanity, sock drawers, kitchen cabinets, and even looked under the kitchen sink. No luck, only the standard over-the-counter drugs. What he needed was some good old fashioned penicillin, and for that he would have to make a quick trip into town.

"What happened?" Holly asked groggily. She swung a leg off of the recliner and struggled to get up.

"Whoa," Dillon said. "You need to stay still. You passed out a few minutes ago. Why didn't you tell me your arm was infected?"

"I was hoping it would go away."

"Hope isn't a strategy, Holly. Don't let these things get out of hand. If you're ever injured again, let me know, even something simple like a scratch or a sore tooth." He paced the length of the room. "You need antibiotics immediately. Where's the nearest pharmacy?"

"There's one in town. It'll take you about ten minutes to get there. Well, if you had a car."

"Which we don't."

"Take one of the horses," Holly said. "You can ride can't you?"

"Once you learn you never forget. Kinda like learning to ride a bike." Dillon's voice and forehead wrinkles rose with each unsure word.

"You've never ridden before, have you?"

"Not since I was a kid."

"Hmm. We have three horses to choose from. Let me think which horse will be best for you." For a few moments, Holly silently made a list of the best attributes of each horse. "Cowboy will be the best one for you. He's dependable, can run like the wind, and he's been trained so nobody can steal him."

"Really? Is there a secret passcode or something?"

"Actually, yes." Holly laughed. "You have to say 'Ride 'em, Cowboy' in a loud voice for him to even take one step. That, plus a good swift kick and he'll take off, so be sure to hang on."

"That's impressive."

Holly paused and put a hand on his arm. "In case something happens to me, I want—"

"Nothing's going to happen to you."

"If it does, I want you to know where we keep the secret stash of guns."

Well, that piqued Dillon's interest. "Oh. I like secret stashes of guns."

"You'll need a Phillips screwdriver. There's one in the drawer to the left of the sink in the kitchen."

Dillon came back with the screwdriver, and Holly instructed him to remove the hardwood planks abutting the wall. "There's a space under the floor. Remove the last board then take up two more. You should see the guns."

Dillon removed the floorboards and carefully set them aside in the order he removed them. When he needed to return them to their original sequence, he'd have an easier job. Peering in the dark space, he spied a Smith & Wesson model 686-7 four inch barreled revolver. He picked it up and checked the seven rounds of .357 magnum ammo in the stainless steel cylinder.

This was better than the buried treasure Mel Fisher found in the shipwrecked *Nuestra Senora de Atocha* and *Santa Margarita,* Spanish galleons sunk off the coast of the Florida Keys during a hurricane in 1722. Dillon carefully placed the Smith & Wesson on the floor.

Tucked away further under the floor, Dillon found a Marlin .357 Magnum Cowboy lever action rifle with an 18-inch barrel. The tubular magazine held nine rounds, and the blue steel rifle had been fitted with a sling.

Not to be disappointed, because a rifle without ammo

is like a swimming pool without water, he found twenty boxes each holding fifty rounds of Winchester 145 grain silvertip hollow points. Somebody knew their business. This type of ammo fed flawlessly in lever action guns and packed a good punch. A .357 magnum bullet out of a rifle had more foot pounds of energy than a .44 magnum revolver had at the muzzle.

Dillon noted the actions of the lever guns and the revolver were smooth from lots of use. They were clean and well cared for, with unscratched muzzles indicating that they would still be accurate. He picked up the Marlin and cranked the lever. Visions of Chuck Conners as the *Rifleman* flashed through his mind and a knowing smile came to his face.

Dillon fiddled with the guns some more, admiring them for what they were: perfectly crafted instruments that only a firearms enthusiast could understand.

"I think I know now what that guy was looking for," Dillon said.

"He didn't find it, did he?"

"Fortunately for us, he didn't. Who knew your parents had a stash of guns?" Holly let out a big breath. "Only close friends and..."

"And who?"

"Cole Cassel."

"How does *he* know?"

"Him and my dad used to talk guns and go target practicing. I'm guessing Cole never forgot about that."

"Asshole," Dillon said. He paced the floor. "He didn't waste any time. How did he beat us back here?" he wondered out loud.

"I don't know," Holly said. "When he was shooting at you, do you think he knew who you were?"

Dillon thought about that. "Probably not. I doubt he could see my face clearly from where he was."

"But he did see us together in the courthouse garage."

"Did you tell him anything about our professional relationship or talk to him about me?"

"No."

"Then he wouldn't know that we are together."

"But he does know that I'm back," Holly said.

"And that won't make it safe here for you."

"I'm not letting Cole or anybody push me around."

Holly instructed Dillon to retrieve Cowboy from the pasture and to bring him up to the house. She told him the saddle and the other equipment were in the barn.

"Can you saddle a horse?"

"I'll figure it out. How do I know which one is Cowboy?"

"Use the magic phrase. He'll come to you. I told you he's smart." As Holly watched him leave, there was a minor detail she left out concerning Cowboy. Better let Dillon figure that out on his own, or better yet, experience it. Holly couldn't help but laugh.

After Cowboy had been saddled, with Holly's help, she stood on the front porch with Buster by her side, telling Dillon which roads to take, the landmarks to be on the watch for, and about how long it would take him to reach the town.

Sitting atop Cowboy, Dillon told Holly to rest while he was gone, not do any work, and be sure she stayed hydrated. And to keep Buster inside since he might try to follow him.

"And don't lift anything or raise your bad arm over your head."

"I promise, I won't," Holly said.

Dillon clumsily held the reins in his hands, trying to encourage Cowboy in the right direction. Cowboy neighed and shook his head. After several frustrating moments, Dillon asked, "What do I need to do to get him to move?"

"The magic phrase. Remember?"

"Oh, right," Dillon said. "Ride 'em, Cowboy!"

With that instruction Cowboy did what horses do best, he ran. Long legs galloped along the road, dust kicking up behind him, running until he and Dillon were out of Holly's sight.

The speed and ease with which Cowboy ran surprised Dillon and he held on to the reins for dear life. Soon, he would be doing something else to keep his life.

Chapter 27

Cowboy ran for a while then slowed to a steady trot. Holly had told Dillon not to run him for too long since the horse wasn't used to running for long distances. They passed pastures full of cattle, abandoned cars and trucks, windmills, stock tanks, and pristine land that hadn't succumbed to the scalpel of civilization.

As Dillon rode it gave him ample time to think about his daughter Cassie, hoping against hope that she was still alive. Having a daughter that needed him gave him purpose in life, knowing he had to go find her. As soon as he returned with the antibiotics for Holly, he'd pack a bag and start the search for his daughter. A father should protect his daughter regardless of how old she was or where she was, and Dillon would search for her until his dying breath.

The sound of another galloping horse interrupted Dillon's thoughts, and he kept a watchful eye on the approaching rider. Dillon held his position as the rider came closer, thinking someone must be in a hurry to ride that fast.

"Hi, neighbor," the man said. He hocked a mouthful

of spit. "That's a fine horse you have." He licked his parched lips, and picked at something in his scalp.

Dillon noted the nervous movements and stunted speech, suspiciously eyeing the side holster holding a gun that bulged under the man's light jacket.

"Afternoon," Dillon replied.

"I'm Lance Crawford," the man said. He sidled up to Cowboy and patted him on the side. Cowboy's eyes grew wide and he swung his head around, nostrils flaring. The horse took a step to the side.

"Dillon Stockdale."

"You from around here?" Lance asked. "I'm actually from up the road," he said. He hooked a thumb.

Dillon wasn't quite sure how to answer the question. The guy had a strange look about him, not exactly a rancher type by the clothes he was wearing. Dillon didn't know a lot of ranchers, but having the head of a snake tattoo peek out from under the cuff on his sleeve surely wasn't a good sign. Besides, a rancher wouldn't be as pale as this guy was.

Taking a chance, Dillon said, "I've got a place down the road." He jerked his head in the direction he came from.

"Ah," Lance said. "The Stockdale place. I heard about that."

A knowing smirk almost flashed across Dillon's face, but he resisted the temptation. "That's me."

"Strange times we have now, don't cha think?"

"Yeah. Who would've thought the world would change on an October day?"

"Go figure," Lance said.

"Well, nice to meet you," Dillon said. "I'm in a hurry and need to get into Hemphill before it gets dark, so if you don't mind, I'll—"

"Town's closed up."

"Doesn't matter. I'll find what I need."

"What's that?" Lance asked.

"Supplies," Dillon said flatly. "Like I said, if you don't mind, I'll be on my way."

"Actually, I do mind," Lance said.

That wasn't something Dillon expected.

Lance reined in his horse and stepped away from Cowboy. His black eyes narrowed to those of a predator's. He tried to position his horse in front of Cowboy, but the horse didn't like the move. He snorted once and stamped the ground.

"I'm going into town," Dillon repeated.

"In due time, neighbor. First, you'll need to pay a toll. In case you haven't heard, there's a new government in town and I've been assigned this road. Anyone that travels on it has to pay me. In return, I'll protect you and your place, and you can come and go as you please. Since paper money looks like it's been devalued, I'll take your horse as payment."

"This isn't exactly the Sam Houston Tollway, and you're not exactly a representative of the toll authority."

Although the exact meaning of the statement escaped Lance's working brain cells, he knew it was a challenge. A fly buzzed Lance and he shooed it away. He swallowed audibly. A dove flew across the road, its wings whistling, and a breeze rustled the dry grass on the side of the road. For some reason Lance felt empty inside, and the blue sky opened up, the trees swaying in the wind. He had never noticed these things before. The Boss said it would be easy. Go out to the road, claim it as your own, and the country folk would obey. If the Boss said it, it must be true.

Both men stood very still.

Cowboy swished a fly that was buzzing his rear.

Lance Crawford wasn't used to being challenged, so this stranger's calm attitude disconcerted him. While he might be bluffing like Lance was, there was something in the way the man talked that meant he would back up what he said.

If Lance went back empty handed, the Boss wouldn't take too kindly to his failure. He had been told to get a horse. What for, he didn't know; people didn't question the Boss. He might get beaten, or worse, a bullet in the back. He'd seen the Boss's henchmen in action before and it wasn't a pretty sight. Maybe he should draw his gun right here, right now, catching Stockdale by surprise. Lance could drag his body off into the bushes, and in a day or two the wild hogs would have torn him to pieces. The only evidence of him passing this way would be a few shreds of clothing.

On the other hand, he thought about reaching for his snub-nosed 38 Special, a poor choice in a weapon that went along with other poor choices Lance had made lately. The chance of getting off a good shot wasn't in Lance's favor. It had been a while since he had target practiced and when he did, the targets never shot back. Lance might not win the gun battle. If he accidentally hit and killed the horse, he'd be going back emptyhanded, and that certainly wouldn't be any good, so when Dillon said, "Okay, you can have the horse," Lance about shit in his pants. The Boss was right, these country folk were pussies.

"Why thank you," Lance said. "I think we're gonna get along real good."

Dillon dismounted Cowboy and stepped back. "Go ahead. He's your horse now."

"Stay back," Lance said. His bravado was rising now. "And don't make any fast moves."

"Whatever you say. You're the boss."

"That's right, I am." Lance mounted Cowboy, took the reins in one hand, the reins to his horse in the other. With the heels of his boots, he kicked Cowboy, prodding him to move.

169

Cowboy did nothing.

"Come on, let's go," Lance ordered. He pulled tighter on the reins and kicked harder. The horse held steadfast.

"Giddy up!" Lance kicked Cowboy again. Lance didn't have much respect or use for horses, considering them dumb beasts, so as he was trying to get Cowboy to move, he didn't notice Dillon positioning himself behind the horse.

Dillon couldn't help but to snicker. Holly was right. The magic phrase was needed.

"What's wrong with this damn horse? Is there some sort of secret code to get this horse to move?" Lance asked.

"Actually, there is," Dillon said. His voice was low and to the point. "And since there's a new government in town, I think I'll put into effect an old law. Stealing horses is a hanging offense, and I'm commissioning a new name for the law now. I think I'll call it Stockdale's Law."

"Huh?" Lance was dumbfounded. "Hanging?" Lance hadn't counted on any of this. It was supposed to have been easy.

"That big oak over there," Dillon said pointing to the century old tree. "Looks like it'll work."

Lance turned around and when he did, he was facing the barrel of a Glock. His thighs quivered and a little pee dribbled out, staining the front of his pants.

"Put your hands in the air, and if you make any quick moves, I'll put a bullet right through your heart. You'll be dead before you hit the ground."

Lance did as he was told and put his hands in the air. He thought quickly about his predicament and about going back empty handed to the Boss. Lance was what people called a "slow learner," and had been marked at a young age where it was easier to put him in remedial classes than actually try to help him. Critical thinking was a skill Lance had not been schooled in, so when he dropped his hands to dismount, he made a fateful decision to reach for his gun.

He was indeed dead before he hit the ground. The hollow point from Dillon's gun had seen to that.

Standing over Lance's body, the pavement darkening from a crimson stain, Dillon pondered what to do. He had already wasted enough time and now the sun was sliding behind the horizon. Seeing that Lance had tried to kill him made Dillon's decision easier. He dragged the body off the road and rolled the corpse into the ditch.

Dillon looked at the horse, decided not to keep it, so with a slap and a yell, the horse took off running down the road.

Twenty minutes later, Dillon came up to the outskirts of the town. Shacks at first with unkempt lawns, old cars jacked-up on bricks, tires missing. The hood of a car was propped up, broken children's toys scattered about.

A man sat on a front porch swing of a house that hadn't seen a woman's care or a new coat of paint in ages. A dingy muscle shirt stretched across the man's beer-bloated belly. A chained dog barked.

Further Cowboy trotted, past a convenience store, windows shattered, the store looted, boxes of macaroni and bags of potato chips knocked haphazardly on the floor.

The laundromat sat empty and dark this Thursday night, no crying babies clamoring for their mothers busily folding clothes. A gas station no longer had the comforting energy of cars and patrons busily going about their business pumping gas and buying cigarettes or candy.

A darkened stoplight swayed and creaked in the breeze, no need to flash green and red lights for cars that didn't work.

A man wearing a black hoodie and baggy pants peddled a fast bike past Dillon. He threw a curious look at Dillon and the horse as if he had never seen a man riding a horse.

Without streetlights and houses lit or florescent bulbs illuminating parking lots, it was dark.

A cloud floated past the full moon, casting long shadows over the land.

The steady beat of Cowboy's clattering hooves upon the blacktop was the only sound on the deserted highway.

A police car sat empty in front of the grocery store, the tires flattened. The automatic sliding doors had been pried open, a bar wedged between the glass and the frame. A looter holding a burlap bag like a hobo ran out of the store and ducked behind a car at the sound of the approaching horse.

Dillon kept his hand on his Glock, ready in case he had to use it again.

By the light of a flickering candle, a shadowy shape in the grocery store moved from aisle to aisle, pushing a shopping cart filled to the brim with canned food, diapers, toiletries, and anything non-perishable.

Up ahead the pharmacy sign loomed dark, and Dillon slowed Cowboy to a walk, approaching the store with caution. Coming up to the front entrance, Dillon dismounted and loosely tied the reins to a bicycle port next to an overflowing trash can. He tugged on the straps on his backpack, tightening them.

He walked into the dark store and ducked behind a row of body lotions of various scents advertised by airbrushed models with glowing skin and red lips. For a brief moment he thought about getting Holly a tube of lipstick. Nah, maybe another time.

A noise in the back caught his attention and he

crouched lower, his Glock steady in his hand. Unafraid of darkness, Dillon knew it would conceal him, as much at it would conceal the unknown. Darkness was his best friend when needed.

Keeping low to the floor, he crept along the aisle of body lotions, careful not to trip on the unwanted items looters had pilfered through. When he came to the end, he jumped across to the next aisle which happened to be the personal care aisle of deodorants and shampoos. Taking advantage of the situation, he stuffed deodorant and bottle of shampoo in his pocket. He spied a pack of disposable razors and reached for it until he realized it would make too much noise.

He heard the noise again. Someone shuffling several aisles away.

Dillon wound his way to the back of the store where the milk and frozen goods had been kept in a working cooler.

He quickly jutted his head around the aisle, trying to get a look at the person loading a soggy frozen dinner into a shopping cart. In the dark light Dillon had trouble discerning the person. Maybe a looter who was hungry. Still, he couldn't be too careful.

"Stop!" Dillon shouted.

The person screamed and dropped the formerly frozen macaroni and cheese to the floor.

"Don't move and put your hands in the air! If you make one move I'll put a bullet through your head. Understand?"

The person stood frozen.

Dillon kept aim on the person and when he got closer, he realized his Glock was on a child. "Turn around."

The child turned around and faced Dillon. The waif of a girl with pleading eyes looked at Dillon.

"How old are you?"

Too frightened to answer, the girl stood there, her

eyes as big as a moon.

"I'm not going to hurt you. How old are you?"

"Ten."

"What are you doing here? Don't you know it's dangerous out here? Where are you parents?"

"I don't have a dad. My mom is home sick. She told me to go to the pharmacy and get her medicine."

"What's wrong with your mom?"

"I don't know. She said she has a fever and needed anti...um, anti..."

"Antibiotics." Dillon pondered that, scratching his beard, itchy from not shaving in days. "Did you find any?"

"I didn't know where to look, so I thought I'd get some food." The child nervously glanced away. "Am I in trouble? You're not going to take me to jail are you?"

"No. I'm here to get antibiotics too. What's your name?"

"Anna Cooper."

"Okay, Anna Cooper," Dillon said, "you stick next to me. I don't want to you getting hurt. Pretend you're my shadow. Can you do that?"

Anna nodded.

"Good. The medicine is behind the counter at the back of the store."

Anna followed Dillon as instructed, as close as she could get without stepping on his boots.

Plastic bottles littered the floor, and the shelves were nearly empty. The cash register had been smashed on the floor, the drawer empty. Dillon stood still a moment.

"What are you doing?" Anna asked.

"Thinking," Dillon said. "Anna I need you to help me. See those bins?" He motioned to the wall behind the counter. "I need you to take the paper bags in the bins, open them, and put the bottles on the counter. Can you do that?"

"I think so."

"Good. We'll go by the alphabet, so you start with A, and I'll start at Z."

Dillon picked Anna up and hoisted her over the counter, surprised at how light she was. If he hadn't asked her how old she was, he would have guessed about seven. Even so, the kid had guts, either that or the mom was nutty as a pecan.

Dillon opened the last bin and tore off the paper package, reached in, and retrieved the bottle of pills. Scanning it, he decided not to keep it, thinking it must have been something for high blood pressure. Methodically, he went through each bag. Fortunately, the looters hadn't bothered with the alphabetized bins since all were full. Some of the medicine he decided to keep and quickly stuffed them in his backpack. He recognized the brand names, seeing that pharmaceutical companies advertised them on TV as if they were soft drinks. The usual maladies advertised: high cholesterol, allergy, insomnia, depression, osteoporosis, migraine, and others. He decided to keep the migraine medicine. He could use that as barter if he needed to. He had gone through about a fourth of the alphabet when he came across pain medicine, deciding to keep that. The other folks, well, he figured they would succumb to their diseases without refills.

"How you doing over there, Anna?" Dillon said after noticing she hadn't made much progress.

"I'm okay," Anna said. She carefully pried open the stapled bag so as not to tear it.

"Just rip off the top and don't worry about it. We need to hurry."

"What do I do with the bag?"

"Throw it on the floor."

"But that's littering."

"Anna, it doesn't matter. Just put the bottles on the

counter as fast as you can."

"Alright." She sounded defeated. "I'm hungry. Do you have anything to eat?"

"I'll get you something after we're finished."

"A hamburger?"

"I don't know about that, but I'll get you something good."

Fifteen minutes later Dillon had gone through all the bottles. He tossed the Viagra, Detrol, Humira, Crestor away. If he didn't recognize the general name, he tossed those too.

Anything ending in 'cillin' he kept, as in amoxicillin or penicillin, also anything ending in 'xacin' and 'cycline'. In all, he found eight bottles of ciprofloxacin, commonly known as Cipro, three bottles of tetracycline, and two each of cefadroxil and Macrobid, the latter for UTIs.

Anna had only managed to open the packagers in the bins marked A,B, C, and D, for a total of about fifty bottles. Dillon decided not to waste anymore time, so he scooped all of them into his backpack.

"Come on," Dillon said. "We have to get going."

"I haven't gone through everything yet," Anna said.

"Doesn't matter. We have to go. I found what I needed."

On the way out, Dillon grabbed a first aid kit, bandages, anti-itch cream, peanut butter and jam, a loaf of wheat bread, disposable razors, several packages of dental floss, toothpaste, and soap. Dillon instructed Anna to stay behind him, and he went out the same way he went in, past where he saw the lipstick. On a whim, he grabbed a tube of lipstick and stuffed it in his pocket.

Coming to the glass paneled front, he stood behind the wall and scanned the parking lot and street. It had gotten darker. In the distance, he heard voices.

Dillon bent down on one knee. "Anna, have you ever ridden a horse?"

"No."

"A bike?"

"Yes."

"Good, riding a horse is like riding a bike, only a little bumpier. We're going to walk out the store and I want you stay behind me. In case something happens, here is one bottle of medicine for your mother. He unzipped her backpack and put the medicine in, along with the peanut butter and bread. "If anything happens, I want you to run as fast as you can, all the way to your house and don't look back, no matter what you hear. Understand?"

Anna nodded.

"Before we go, tell me where you live."

After Anna told Dillon where she lived, giving him directions as best she could, Dillon told her that he would get on the horse first. She would ride behind him and hold on to him with all she had. "Don't be scared. Pretend you're a pioneer girl."

"Like Annie Oakley?"

Dillon smiled. "Just like her. Good girl, let's go."

Chapter 28

You'd think riding a horse in Texas was a common sight, but it really wasn't, regardless of how the movies portrayed Texas. While there are riding horses, it's mostly done for pleasure and competitions in rodeos. Horses used in husbandry work went the way of the buggy whip.

Although the city was small, the sound of hooves on pavement caused people to take notice, because a horse galloping down the street carrying a man with a child wasn't your everyday occurrence.

A couple of shots were fired and Dillon speculated those were celebratory shots, either that or the person firing couldn't hit the broad side of a barn.

It didn't take them long to get to Anna's house. It was a frame house, one story, at one time had been painted white, and from the outside it appeared small, perhaps with a couple of bedrooms, living area, and an eat-in kitchen. Old plastic toys were scattered in the yard, and couple of yard cats skittered away at the sight of Cowboy.

It was dark, and the house looked devoid of life.

178

Fortunately, Dillon had a flashlight he brought from home that had been in a Faraday-type gun safe, where it was protected from the effects of the EMP.

"Anna, take my hand and I'll let you down. I'll take Cowboy to the backyard, so in case anyone gets an idea to steal him, Cowboy will be safe. I'll come in for a moment to make sure your mom takes her medicine."

Anna slipped down the saddle then skipped up the porch steps and swung open the screen door. It slammed shut with a thud. Dillon loosely tied Cowboy's reins to one of the poles holding up the overhang on the back porch, if you could call it that. It was more like a wide inverted V over concrete steps. He told Cowboy to stay and not go anywhere while the chickens in the backyard coop flapped noisily.

"Mommy, you home? Mommy?"

A weak voice replied, "I'm here on the couch."

"Mommy, I have the medicine you need," Anna said. She reached into the backpack and took out the bottle. "And I've got peanut butter and bread," she said proudly. She handed the bottle of medicine to her mother.

"Sweetie, put the peanut butter and bread in the kitchen and get me a glass of water."

"Okay, Mommy."

Dillon kicked the dirt off his boots on the top concrete step then knocked once before entering the house. The flashlight's beam bounced around the room containing the usual furniture: a sofa, chair, coffee table, a few magazines scattered about, and a boxy TV on a stand in the corner.

"Anna? Who's this?"

"He's a friend. He helped me find the medicine for you."

"Evening, ma'am," Dillon said. "I wanted to make sure Anna got home safe and that you got the medicine you needed."

"Thank you. I'm Dorothy Cooper. Please come in and sit down. Anna, would you get this nice man a drink of water?"

"That's not necessary," Dillon said, "I have water, and you'll need to keep whatever you have."

"Sweetie, would you get me a pillow, please?"

Anna scurried to the bedroom to fetch a pillow.

"Thank you so much for getting the antibiotics for me," Dorothy said to Dillon. "The nurse called in the prescription right before the electricity went out. I stopped by the pharmacy, but they said their computers were down and that I'd have to come back tomorrow. As you know, tomorrow came and went, and no electricity. Oh, I'm sorry, I didn't catch your name."

"Dillon Stockdale."

Dorothy's face relaxed into a worried scowl, and she swallowed audibly. Her gaze swiveled from the front door then back to Dillon. "Turn that flashlight off."

"Is everything okay?" Dillon asked. He sensed the immediate change in her demeanor when he said his name.

"Turn it off."

Dillon flicked the flashlight off. "What's wrong?" he asked.

"Are you the Dillon Stockdale from Houston that was prosecuting Cole Cassel?"

"That's me. How did you know that?"

"Everybody knows Cole and what a mean son of a bitch he is."

"What does that have to do with anything?" Dillon asked.

"Cole is back."

"What's he doing back here? How did he get here so fast?
Dillon asked.

"He probably stole a car. He's good at that."

180

Dillon nodded. "He's done time for grand theft auto."

"You know this is his home turf, don't you?" Dorothy asked.

"I learned it the other day," Dillon said.

"Animals always come back to what they know. He's taking control of the city, street by street. Everybody is afraid of him, and he's got spies everywhere. If any of them see you here, they'll kill me."

Dillon now understood why her demeanor had changed. "Dorothy, do you know if Cole is driving an old white truck, possibly a Ford?"

"I heard that he is."

"What else have you heard?"

"Talk is that he's already killed the sheriff and two deputies, and word got around that if anyone helps any of his enemies, he'll kill that person and their entire family. So you see why you need to get out of here."

Dillon nodded.

"I've also heard he's sent out his henchmen to collect tolls on the country roads around here."

"Someone already tried to collect from me."

"What happened?" Dorothy asked.

Dillon lowered his voice. "Let's just say the toll didn't get paid." Dillon paced the floor. "Do you know Holly Hudson by any chance?"

"We went to high school together."

"Small world. Do you know where her parents' place is?"

"Yes, most everyone knows where their spread is. They died though. I thought it had been sold."

"Holly kept the house," Dillon said. "Listen to me, things are going to get really bad really quickly. If you run out of food, you and your daughter can go to Holly's place, but don't tell anybody."

"I appreciate that," Dorothy said. "When electricity comes back on, we'll be okay."

Dillon shook his head. "It will be a long time before electricity comes back on. There was an EMP that hit the United States, probably several."

"What's an EMP?"

"I don't have time to explain. If you have a gun, get it, and keep it handy. And those chickens you have in the coop outside? Those are worth more than gold. At night, bring them in and put them in an enclosed space, maybe a closet. Line the floor with paper. And if you have egg layers—"

"I do."

"Then definitely bring them in the house every night, starting tonight. You'll need the eggs yourself, and you can use them as barter. Money will soon be worthless."

"We're okay for a little while here. Good luck to you. I'm going to have to ask you to leave now. You understand?"

"I do," Dillon said. "The offer is still open for you and your daughter to come out to Holly's place."

"Thank you," Dorothy said. "Now please—"

"I'm leaving now."

Chapter 29

The ride back to Holly's place was uneventful. When Dillon passed by the ditch where Cole's henchman lay dead, Cowboy must have sensed it by the way he hesitated and flared his nostrils when he trotted by.

Taking Cowboy to the barn, Dillon removed the riding equipment, hanging up the saddle, bit and bridle, and placing the pad on an old workbench. He put out some feed for Cowboy and the other horses then ran to the house.

Flinging open the front door, Dillon was greeted by a warning bark until Buster recognized his owner. Buster came over to him, wiggling all over and thumping his tail. Dillon reached down and scratched Buster behind his ears.

He set his backpack on a chair and went to the kitchen to pour a glass of water. Fortunately, there was still some water pressure, though the trickle of water from the faucet indicated the pressure was falling.

He went to Holly, who was still on the sofa. In the dim moonlight filtering in from the windows, he stood there a minute looking at her, admiring her tenacity and ability to push through the 150 mile bike ride from Houston to her ranch, especially injured. Learning about her history with Cole Cassel was an eye-opener, and now that Cole was back in town, Holly would be a sitting duck if she stayed here at the house by herself. He had planned on leaving first thing in the morning. Now he wasn't so sure about that. He'd play it by ear regarding when he would leave. With everything going on, he hadn't had much time to think about his daughter. He wondered how she was, where she was, and how he would find her. There was a lot of wide open country between East Texas and New Orleans, rivers to cross, towns to navigate, desperate people. With too many unknowns, he knew he had a big job in front of him.

Nudging her arm, Dillon said, "Holly, you need to wake up. I've got antibiotics for you."

Holly opened her eyes a slit and yawned. "You're back. What time is it?"

"Probably midnight. Can you sit up?"

"I think so," Holly said. She rubbed her eyes.

"Here," Dillon said, handing her the opened bottle of antibiotics. "Take one now, and try to drink as much water as possible."

Taking a pill, Holly washed it down with a big gulp of water.

"These are the strongest ones I could find. They should start working soon. I'm guessing you'll feel better in the morning."

"I think I'll go back to sleep. I'll stay here on the sofa."

"Wherever you want to sleep is fine by me. It's your house. Sure you don't want to sleep on your bed?"

"The sofa is good." Holly briskly rubbed her arms. "I didn't realize it's so chilly. Can you get me that throw over there?" she asked, pointing to the chair in the

184

corner.

Dillon retrieved the throw blanket and draped it loosely over Holly. "If you need anything, call me. I'll leave the bedroom door open."

In the morning, Holly woke to sunlight streaming into the room. She was surprised at how long she had slept and how restfully. It had been a while since she had slept so well. Maybe it was because of the country air, or the fact she was tired, or that her body needed rest to heal. Regardless of how she tried to rationalize it, she couldn't help but to think she slept well because Dillon was in the house. It had been a long time since she felt safe.

She listened to the chorus of chirping birds filling the quiet morning through the open windows. In the city, she had never taken the time to listen to the birds, mainly because the windows were sealed shut what with central heat and air and all. That and the fact it wasn't safe to leave the windows open. Plus there was something comforting about listening to the whir of central air-conditioning, the steady hum of cars outside, or merely the general beat of civilization. She had taken all that for granted up until a few days ago.

Although Holly couldn't recognize the different songbird tunes, she did recognize the rhythmic tapping of a woodpecker.

Sitting up, she threw off the throw blanket and ran her fingers through her hair. What she wanted was a long, hot bath, clean hair, and a change of clothes. The bandage on her arm smelled a bit gamey, indicating it was high time her wound needed a good washing.

"You're up," Dillon said, walking into the room, Buster right behind him. "You look a million miles away. Penny for your thoughts?"

The question took Holly by surprise, and she wasn't

quite sure how to answer that. Be truthful or make something up? She decided on the former. "I was thinking about air-conditioning."

Dillon laughed. "Enjoy the memories because it will be a long time before AC works again." He held a plate of biscuits and scrambled eggs. "You hungry?"

"As a matter of fact, I am. Did you cook that yourself?"

"I ordered room service," he deadpanned.

Holly laughed.

"Come on into the kitchen and let's eat," Dillon said.

He set the plate of biscuits and scrambled eggs on the table, poured canned peaches into a bowl, and asked Holly if she would like some coffee.

"I'm impressed. How did you make all this, especially the coffee?" Holly asked.

"It's camp coffee, your specialty. Remember? The morning after coffee?"

"We were supposed to forget about that," Holly said.

"While you were sleeping I gathered up a few eggs from the chicken coop, started a fire, and boiled water. The coffee I found in the pantry still smelled good, so I added some grounds, let it settle, and voila, you have coffee now. Be careful because not all the grounds settled, so watch out for the ones floating on top. The peaches were still in date."

"My neighbor canned those."

"The pantry is stocked full of canned peaches and pickled beets and cucumbers. I also found a basket of heirloom seeds. In a month, there will be a good crop of pecans. With a little work, we'll be able to grow vegetables."

Holly took a bite of scrambled eggs, mulling over the word 'we'. It surprised her, not quite knowing if that was a slipup, or if Dillon meant to say that, especially since he was a masterful orator. She had heard him enough in the courtroom to know that he chose his words carefully. To her, it indicated he considered them a team. Maybe not a couple, but a team. It also indicated Dillon was planning on staying awhile, not simply passing through as a place to hang his hat for a night, as Holly had originally thought. He had gone to great trouble to get her antibiotics, postponing his trip by a day for when he had to leave to search for his daughter. She had taken up enough of his precious time.

"Dillon," she said, "you really don't need to waste anymore time here with me. Your daughter needs you more than I do. I'll be alright here by myself. Buster can stay here with me."

Dillon put down his fork. He kneaded his forehead, thinking, took a swallow of coffee. "Not with Cole Cassel back in town."

Holly stared at him for a long second. She couldn't believe what she heard. "How do you know that for sure?"

Dillon told Holly about the child he helped at the pharmacy and how he got her home safely. It was then he learned that Cole had come back to town.

"He's already killed the sheriff and his two deputies. I also learned that he drives an old white truck."

"Who told you all this?"

"Some woman, her name was…" he snapped his fingers searching for her name, "Dorothy Cooper."

"About my age?"

Dillon nodded.

"Short, brown hair, big eyes?"

"That pretty much describes her. Do you know her?"

"We went to school together, starting in kindergarten. There was a bunch of girls Dorothy and I were friends with. Sometime around middle school, we grew apart. I had a couple of classes with her in high school, but we didn't really hang around each other that much. We went different ways. I left to go to college, she stayed here."

"She looks like she's had a hard life," Dillon said.

"She has a kid?"

"Yes, a brave little girl."

Holly got up and took her dishes to the sink. She scraped the leftover biscuits and scrambled eggs into Buster's bowl. "No need to let food go to waste. You don't mind if Buster gets table food, do you?"

"No, not at all. He'll need the extra calories," Dillon said watching Buster scarf down the food.

"That was Cole here yesterday, wasn't it?" Holly said, the realization hitting her about what he did. "That bastard! He was trying to kill us, wasn't he?" Holly paced in front of the sink and cabinets, her anger building. "Why would he do that?"

"Because he wanted this place, knowing it was empty. He knew you were in Houston and probably thought you would stay there. Guess he didn't count on me coming with you."

Holly dropped her shoulders. "He killed Hector, didn't he?"

"Probably."

"That son of a bitch. Hector never did anything to anybody. What a waste."

"Does Hector have any family around here?"

"None that I know of. Maybe a brother somewhere. He didn't talk about his family much."

Rising from his chair, Dillon went over to Holly. He stood facing her, and for the first time Holly felt at ease being so close to him. Dillon took her by the arms and she was keenly aware of how warm and strong his hands felt, and she was surprised at her reaction. Their relationship, if you could call it that, was progressing backwards from the usual meet, get to know each other before the physical part happened. Getting the physical part out of the way had been first.

Holding each other's gaze, the moment became heady and Dillon could have sworn she was looking at him with those same doe eyes she had the other night. He released the hold he had on her arms and backed away.

"Holly, you can't stay here alone. It's not safe anymore, especially since Cole knows you are here. Is there anyone you can stay with in town?"

"No. I've lost touch with everyone." Holly scratched her head. "My parents had some good friends that have nearby ranches but I wouldn't feel right imposing on them. They will be in the same situation as we are in. Food will be scarce, water too. I don't want to be a burden on anyone."

"Then there's only one solution," Dillon said. "You're coming with me."

Chapter 30

Holly stood there, stunned. She knew he was right because staying here by herself there was no way she was adequately prepared to defend her homestead. She had a ranch to run, crops to plant, food preparation... Then there was the matter of fuel. So many things to consider. In normal times, she wouldn't have had an issue, all it would take would be to hire a couple of guys, pay them for all the heavy lifting, and life would be good.

Cole could come back at any time, day or night, catch her off guard or when she was asleep, and she'd be a goner. The things her parents had worked for all their lives would be in the hands of a murderer.

On the other hand, if she vacated the ranch, anyone could come in and occupy the place, because the expression *possession is nine-tenths of the law* would trump any law on the books during times like these. The types of people who would squat on a deserted homestead wouldn't be concerned with a step-by-step checklist regarding the proper protocol of squatter's rights.

New laws would be formed by those that were stronger, those who would conquer, settling scores with the laws of the old west that were swift in dispensing justice. Holly might have been well educated in modern laws, court procedures, and loopholes, but the law of the gun ruled now and she knew it.

"Well?" Dillon asked.

"I'll come with you."

"It's a wise choice. Thank you for not protesting."

"I know my limitations, and staying here alone wouldn't be a good idea. What do you need me to do to help you get ready?"

For the next several hours Dillon and Holly prepared for the trip. There was food to pack, like salt and nonperishable items, along with cooking utensils, tasks he gave to Holly not because he was a chauvinist, rather she would be better at that and know where the items were located.

Holly was better at some things, while Dillon at others, and besides, now was not the time to argue about who did what better.

Holly seemed to understand Dillon's non-verbal way of thinking, and she went about the task of collecting food and utensils with incredible finesse.

After she had finished Dillon complimented her on the choices and the ability to pack the items into the bag he gave her.

Next on the list included water filtration and sterilization, clothes, medical supplies, weapons and ammo, sleeping bag, a poncho if it rained, so many items to consider.

Fortunately, some of the items could be used by both of them, such as a tent and cooking utensils, so that provided room for other necessary items. Dillon packed most of the firearms, meticulously counting ammo and magazines they would need. So as not to leave Holly out in the cold in case they were separated, he packed her a cache of ammo as well.

Holly packed clothes and necessary hygiene items such as soap and dental floss, because it would take up less space than a toothbrush and toothpaste. Besides, as gross as it may sound, dental floss could be reused. Good oral hygiene was necessary because a toothache could result in a serious infection which would migrate to the sinuses, then to the brain, resulting in a hard death.

Dillon rummaged around the house and barn looking for anything useful, Buster right along with him, sensing both Dillon's and Holly's rising anxiety level and purposeful movements. Buster had seen this before when Dillon prepared for a trip, and while the dog could not understand where they were going or why, he understood it was important.

A new adventure would soon begin, and for a city dog used to sleeping all day, his new life had become invigorating. It was exhilarating to be needed, to be useful. He was doing what a dog should do: be a companion and use his superior canine abilities to alert his pack to danger. Buster scanned the woods for any movement, kept his nose close to the ground searching for snakes or other vermin, tasted the air for unusual wafting scents, and lastly, at night stood guard as a sentry, listening to the sounds of the night.

Little did the dog understand, but this new purpose in life and newfound determination to live as his canine ancestors did would one day protect the viability of his new pack.

Chapter 31

Dillon decided it was best to wait a couple of days to let the antibiotics do their work, so his journey to find his daughter was further delayed. He saw to it that Holly rested, ate well, and kept the arm clean.

Three days had passed since Holly started taking the antibiotics, and whenever he touched her arm checking on the wound, his thoughts went back to that first night at his house when she looked at him with doe eyes. It had become the proverbial elephant in the room neither one of them wanted to deal with.

Hell, maybe those goo-goo eyes she made at him wasn't lust after all. Instead of being misty, her eyes could have been glazing over because she was in the throes of a fainting spell.

But she hadn't fainted.

She was the one that leaned into him, pressing herself against him, and what guy wouldn't take that as a clue alluding to something else?

When he wrapped his arms around her, she didn't fight him off, or even squeak a protest. She had done the opposite, holding him tighter. When he picked her up and carried her to the bedroom, setting her down on the bed, it wasn't to tuck her in. The signals she sent him were loud and clear and a foghorn couldn't have been louder.

Then again, he wasn't the one that had a crying fit and needed to be consoled and comforted.

What followed could only be considered unadulterated lust and the need to connect with another human being. If they had been teenagers he might have been tempted to the *don't you want to know what it feels like in case you die tomorrow?* ruse some used to deflower virgins. Or in the case of adults, the possibility tomorrow wouldn't come at all. The sweaty, lustful romp did them both good.

Her reaction the morning after surprised him, and now that they had spent almost a week together he wasn't sure what to think about it. Maybe he was overanalyzing, because he tended to do that with cases. Even the tiniest details had to be thought out, but God Almighty, some women were difficult to figure out.

Trying to push those thoughts out of his mind, Dillon rode further with Cowboy, becoming acquainted with the ranch roads, the natural contours of the land, ponds, and the seasonal branch lined with trees. Knowing the intricacies of the land would come in handy one day. Not only was the ride cathartic, it was mandatory. As he rode down to the branch, he had to weave his way around trees and brush. When he came to the dry creek, Cowboy took the lead and walked along without any prodding. The horse acted like he was taking a walk in the park. Obviously, he knew the country well.

It was quiet and dark under the canopy, only a few lonely rays of sun squeezing through.

Dillon had been riding for over an hour and the time alone had let him clear his thoughts. He decided they would have to leave in the morning. A good night's sleep would do him good and since supplies had been packed, that was one thing he had to check off his to-do list. He had tried to plan for every contingency possible, although what was in store for him, he would never have imagined.

Chapter 32

The trek through the countryside to find Cassie had taken longer than expected. Dillon and Holly had to be careful to skirt cities and other places where an ambush could be possible, so traveling the way the crow flew was next to impossible. Their route tripled their travel time, and by the time they came to the Atchafalaya Basin Bridge, they had already been on horseback for three days, with still more to go before they were in the vicinity where the plane probably went down.

Deciding it was too dangerous to cross the bridge, what with seeing armed people on the bridge who probably wanted a toll to pass, Dillon and Holly turned south.

He couldn't even bring himself to say the word 'crash'. It seemed so final. So deadly.

If Cassie had been injured and was lying somewhere in the wilderness, she'd wouldn't have had a snowflake's chance in Hell. If something had happened to her, Dillon prayed it was quick and merciful.

Going over the various scenarios was too taxing on

Dillon's mental state, so he instead concentrated on something he could control.

A couple of hours later, and as luck would have it, he and Holly came upon a fish camp located on a bayou where an old man was sitting in a rocking chair chewing on a long stem of grass.

"Howdy," Dillon said.

"Howdy," the old-timer replied back. "What brings you this way?"

"I'm looking for my daughter. She was on an airplane that went down somewhere in south Louisiana."

The old man rubbed the stubble on his chin. "About a week ago?"

"Yes."

"I saw a plane about that time. Flying too low, lower than I've ever seen one. I watched it for a while until it disappeared."

"What direction was it going?" Dillon asked.

The old man pointed to the east. "It's going to be a rough ride to where you need to go," the Cajun old-timer said. "A bizness man stumbled through here yesterday, lookin' somethin' poorly. All scratched up. Clothes torn. Nearly fainted from thirst. Said somethin' about he was the only survivor of a plane crash."

Dillon glanced at Holly, who returned an equally deflated expression. "Was he sure he was the only survivor?" Dillon asked.

"That's what he said."

"Where is he now?"

"Left this mornin'. I fed him, gave him some water. Said he was walkin' home."

"Where was home?"

"Dallas."

"Hmm," Dillon said. "He was headed in a different direction than we were."

The old-timer scratched his white beard. "He was

197

real lucky, 'cause where the plane went down, it's bad. Real bad. Swampy, woods and vines so thick you need a machete. Then there's lots of gators. If you catch one, though, it's good eatin'. Bring me some if you come back this way."

"I'll be sure to do that," Dillon said with a chuckle.

"Nuthin' lasts long in the swamp, 'specially bodies," the old-timer said. "Hogs eat 'em, gators, cougars too. I heard one screaming the other night. Sounded like a woman." He shook his head. "You can try to find your daughter, but there won't be nuthin' left of anyone by now. Nature's way of cleanin' things. Won't even be any bones left."

Dillon dismissed the ramblings as the musings of an old man. "Did the man say anything else?"

"Somethin' about a whole team of soccer players was on the plane. He felt bad for them because they was young and was excited about going to some match."

"Soccer players you say?"

"Yes. Why?"

Dillon thought for a moment. "My daughter mentioned something about a plane full of soccer players. That had to be her plane, so if one person survived, there could be others."

"If that's what gets you through your day, so be it." The old-timer paused and looked wistfully at Buster. "My hound dog, Gus, up and died last month. He was a good dog, like that there dog you have. I gave him a proper burial. Back yonder," he pointed, "behind that shed. Didn't want the gators or coons to eat him up. Even carved him a headstone with his name on it. If you don't want that dog I could take him off your hands. I need me another good dog."

Dillon shook his head. "My daughter gave me the dog, so he's got a special place in my heart."

"I understand," the old-timer said.

"Thanks for your help," Dillon said. "We have to get going. My daughter is still out there somewhere."

"Before you go," the old-timer said, "let me get ya somethin' for your dog to eat."

"I appreciate that," Dillon said.

The old-timer hobbled off the rocking chair and hobbled over to the shack. When he came out, he had a ten pound sack of dog food and a handmade fish trap.

"I don't do much fishing anymore, knees and legs are too bad to walk far. This fish trap caught me a fair share of fish in its time. Take it," he said, handing it to Dillon. "It's old, but it still works good. I baited it with hog meat." He explained how to work it, and told Dillon it would come in handy where they were going. "Look for a clearing rimmed by trees about three miles east of here. Go a little further and you'll come upon a lake. It's good fishin' there."

"Thank you," Dillon said. "My dog thanks you too."

The old-timer nodded and bid them a safe trip. "You better get going, get your camp settled, and set your fish traps before it gets dark. The woods aren't forgivin'. You remember that."

Later that day Dillon, Holly, and Buster found the clearing the old man spoke about. Riding further, they found the lake. It was mid-afternoon, and Dillon decided to make camp among a grove of trees not far from the lake. He tied the horses to a tree and left them food to eat. He'd let them graze when he got back.

While Holly went about setting up shelter, Dillon made the short hike to the lake to set out the fish trap.

Coming back to the campsite, he poured Buster a big bowl of dog food. While Buster ate, Dillon sat on a log wondering how long he would need to leave the trap. He was hungry and fresh fish and the protein it provided would do both him and Holly good.

Buster, sitting at Dillon's feet, his head resting on a boot, gazed at his owner, taking in his posture and mood.

"You're a good dog." He reached toward his dog, took a handful of coarse hair and loose skin and massaged his dog's back. "Well, boy, what do you think? Should we stay here or go round up some grub?"

Buster thumped his tail.

"That's what I thought." Dillon debated whether or not to wait until Holly came back from gathering greens. Earlier she told him she had spotted clover and wild persimmons, and a good patch of cattails. It wasn't a chef's salad with all the trimmings, but it would help to fill their bellies and provide vitamins they needed.

Dillon checked the shadows falling on the land. In an hour, the sun would set, so unless he wanted to go hungry, he needed to check the fish traps.

The short hike to the lake would be easier without the horses, so he left them where they were.

Dillon wore an undershirt and a checkered flannel shirt over that. His worn boots kept his feet warm and he had his jeans tucked into the boots.

Deciding he didn't need the outer shirt, he shrugged it off, folded it, and placed it on the log.

He added another log to the fire, poked the embers with a longer stick, placing the log just right so that it wouldn't smother the fire.

Before he left, he found a stick and scribbled the words *checking fish traps* in the dirt. He hoped Holly would see it so she wouldn't worry about him when she returned.

"Come on, Buster," Dillon said. "Let's go get us a mess of fish."

He slung his AK over his shoulder, made sure his Glock was secured in the holster, and set out for the lake. With Buster by his side, Dillon moved through the canopy of trees and vines, his footfalls silent on the spongy earth.

If this had been a normal hunt, during normal times, Dillon would have set out early in the morning before daybreak, when the land was dewy and clean. Buster would have been by his side. They would have stayed out for an hour or so, adhering to state hunting laws. Afterwards, they would have walked a short ways to his truck, where a thermos of hot coffee would be waiting. He'd pour a bowl of water for Buster and share jerky with his dog.

Only a few months ago that's what he had done.

Now? He hunted or fished when he was hungry. He did this to survive, not for leisure.

Dillon and Buster walked on.

Always aware of his surroundings, he glimpsed a wary squirrel perched on a low limb of a cypress tree. The squirrel chattered its displeasure at his presence, yet remained perched on the low limb.

Buster stopped and took the stance of a pointer. The mutt had some good genes in him after all.

"Good boy," Dillon said, praising his dog.

If Dillon had something other than an AK, perhaps a 22, he could have taken a shot at the squirrel, because the AK would have obliterated the squirrel. It would have been a useless shooting and a waste of ammo. The minute amount of meat on a squirrel would barely compensate for the effort and amount of calories expended. What he needed was carbohydrates, and hopefully Holly could find some wild yams.

Dillon passed under the chattering squirrel and continued to where he'd set the fish trap.

They followed an animal trail, patted down by countless trips of four legged creatures. He spotted different types of animal prints, and Buster nosed the ground, checking the scents. There were armadillo, raccoon, turkey, deer, and more wild hog tracks.

Closer to the lake there were crawfish mounds. They bypassed those and continued on. Coming to the edge of the lake, a splash caught his attention and he turned in that direction, spying a couple of turtles on a log.

Buster sensed they had reached their destination. The big dog went over to a fallen tree and sniffed the bare branches. Nosing the length of the tree, he stopped and pawed at the ground, snorted once, and sat down.

"Whatever is in there, we're not going to eat it," Dillon said. "We're after fish, not a skunk, so stay back."

As if understanding, Buster eased away from the tree. Dillon stood at the water's edge, letting his eyes search for a spot to put his AK and his boots. He needed to wade into the water a ways to where the fish traps were and didn't want to get his boots wet or take a chance with the AK. He hadn't seen any evidence of humans so felt safe leaving his AK and boots nearby. Scouting around, he found a sturdy tree where it wasn't too wet and leaned the AK against it.

Buster had a keen sense on who was friendly and who wasn't. He'd smell a person long before Dillon saw anyone.

Although Dillon had stressed over whether or not to take Buster on the trip, leaving him behind to fend for himself had not been an option. Nobody wanted to feed an extra mouth, especially someone else's dog. More especially a 70 pound dog that could eat as much as an adult.

The trip had invigorated Buster. *Brain stimulation* Dillon had called it. It's what dogs were meant to do. To be outside in the natural environment, working or claiming the land, herding livestock, flushing varmints.

There was a light breeze stippling the water, and Dillon scanned in all directions. He took off his boots and socks, placed them on a log, then rolled up his pants. He stepped into the water and slid his feet along the bottom one step at a time, testing the bottom for firmness.

When Buster waded into the water, Dillon pointed at him with a flick of his arm, commanding, "Stay back," using a tone the dog understood.

Buster reluctantly went to the shore, sat down, and whimpered.

"I won't be long," Dillon said. "Stay there." The fish trap, made out of sticks and string, was crude, yet effective, letting the fish in, but not out. Dillon had staked it with a study branch so it wouldn't float away.

Wading in the water, he took his time getting to the trap, trying not to get too wet. Hurrying was a thing of the past, as were a lot of things. The trek to find his daughter had taken him longer than he anticipated, and if he took much longer, he might never find her.

Since she was a child, Dillon had tried to prepare her for various catastrophic scenarios. Living on the Texas Gulf Coast they had bugged in several times due to hurricanes and the resulting power outages.

"It's good experience for when something really bad happens," he told her once.

He had given her strict instructions that if there ever was a crisis that she was to bug in, and hopefully she had heeded his advice. If she rationed food and water from the airplane, she would likely have enough for a month.

If there was one survivor of the plane crash, there would be others. He prayed his daughter was one of them. Yet if she left the crash site, she would have had to find her way out of the swamp, cross inhospitable terrain, and keep to the lowlands away from people.

Wading into the cool, murky water, he wiggled his toes in the silty bottom, relishing the brief pleasure. Maybe later he'd come back with a bar of soap and take a bath, knowing he sure could use one. Riding horseback for days tended to make a person gamey. Maybe he'd even shave, because his beard was itchy. His hair too. He absentmindedly scratched his scalp. A hot shower was a luxury of the past, even a cold shower, and his mind took him—

The water exploded.

A powerful force ripped him off his feet and Dillon fell backwards with a splash, swallowing a mouthful of the sediment laden water.

Buster rose and ran to the edge of the water, barking. Instinct told him to stay back.

Dillon didn't have time to react or to reach for his gun. Adrenaline flooded his bloodstream in the amount of time it took his heart to beat once.

He struggled to the surface and a garbled yell escaped Dillon's lips. He tried to yell again, but was slammed back underwater.

Buster barked furiously at the edge of the lake, long strings of drool hanging from his mouth. He raced back and forth, splashing through the shallows, his underbelly wet with swamp water.

Dillon was thrown to the surface and he spit out the swamp water and gulped air just as he was dragged back under. He held his breath and clawed and pounded at the alligator clamping down on his kneecap and thigh.

It was hard and bony. *Massive.*

He had a brief thought that alligators should be hibernating, or at least so sluggish as not to be a threat.

The alligator violently twisted Dillon and his head hit a stump protruding from the muddy bottom. Again he was thrashed. He didn't know which way was up, but when he felt air on his face, he gulped a breath.

Think!

He was being pulled further into the swamp, into deeper water. The apex predator was trying to drown him. Dillon was loosely aware of Buster barking.

Dillon reached for his Glock. If he could get a good

shot at the alligator, maybe he had a fighting chance. His hand went to the holster, but his gun wasn't there. His hand felt all around. It must have been wrenched loose.

Think!

The death roll started again, the thrashing, the crushing weight, and the thousand pound prehistoric beast had gotten the upper hand.

Dillon hit his head on a log, again. He was disoriented and desperately needed to breathe. He slapped at the water, at the massive jaw crushing his leg. He concentrated on keeping his mouth closed. Inhaling a lung full of water would be the demise of him. How much longer could he hold his breath before he blacked out? Before he died?

Maybe a few seconds he thought.

His heart hammered against his chest, feeling like it was about to explode, while his lungs screamed for air. He struggled desperately to keep from inhaling the murky swamp water.

So this was how it was going to end—alone, in the jaws of a monster alligator in the swamps of Louisiana.

In his adrenaline-charged state, Dillon didn't feel the crushing weight against his leg or the chilling water soaking his soul.

He frantically searched for anything to hold onto, a tree limb, a submerged stump, but all he felt was the cold, leathery skin of the alligator.

Dillon's eyes were shut tight and his lips pressed hard together. He didn't know which way was up to the surface to the air he needed.

With the sensation of his life ebbing away his thoughts became fuzzy, and even though his eyes were closed, stars appeared against the backdrop of his life.

Buster's barks became fainter, echoing, like they were coming from deep within a tunnel.

In one last desperate effort, Dillon thrust his arm into the alligator's mouth, between bone-crunching teeth and the crushing jaw. He stretched, reaching for the soft palate, to rip it out.

His heart pounded.

He needed to breathe...

He kept his mouth clamped shut.

The alligator continued thrashing him.

Water exploded on the surface, mud and murky debris swirling around them.

He felt his life slipping away...everything became eerily silent.

The overpowering need to breathe vanished, and Dillon went limp, his arms swaying in the water. He had no more strength to fight the beast and his body rolled soundlessly in the dark water.

Images of his life came to him, of his wife and daughter, when they were young when the world was different, when the world was safe. Cherished memories flashed before him, ones to be revisited, and an ethereal, spiritual peace enveloped him. Still, he was vaguely aware of the power pummeling his body, of being dragged through the water.

Dillon opened his eyes to a facet of consciousness still refusing to surrender to death, a spark of life flickering in the dank, murky waters. His dying body violently convulsed in a last ditch effort, struggling to live, an automatic survival response.

He had a strange sensation of walking or floating. He couldn't quite understand where he was, everything was so hazy and bright. His wife, Amy, was beside him. She was smiling and laughing. He hadn't seen her in so long, and he ached to be reunited with her, even if it had to be in death. She was so young and pretty. Her sun-kissed hair cascaded down her shoulders.

She held out a hand, motioning for him to take it,

whispering words he couldn't understand.

He reached for her hand, eager to thread his fingers through hers.

To touch her once more.

She was just out of reach. Inches away. Then her face relaxed, and a curious sadness stretched across her beautiful features. She turned her back on him, walking away.

"Come back," he said.

She looked over her shoulder at him, her eyes downcast...

He ran to her. "Don't go," he said. "I want to stay with—"

Boom!

Silence.

Boom!

The violent sounds jolted him back to reality and to the pain of dying.

He'd never imagined dying like this. After everything he had been through, after fighting to live for so long, this was it, and nobody would know what happened to him. Worst of all, he would never fulfill his promise to find her.

He shuddered once, his body fell limp and he submitted to the blackness closing around him.

Holly had seen Dillon's writing in the dirt, and decided to surprise him with the bounty she had found. Walking in the direction he had gone, she picked up the pace when Buster started barking. After being around the dog for a week, she knew he wasn't one to bark unnecessarily.

Running through the thick underbrush, she hadn't felt the briars scraping her arms or the branches slapping her face, all she could think was that something was terribly wrong.

Bursting through the clearing she came upon Buster running frantically at the water's edge. Seeing her, he ran to her with a desperate look in his eyes she had never seen before. It was then she saw the alligator rolling Dillon over and over in the water.

She took a quick look around for any type of weapon, perhaps a sturdy stick or a rock, and it was then she saw the AK propped up against a tree. Holly sprinted to it, and recalling Dillon's handling of the weapon, she picked it up, took the safety off, sighted it and fired a practice round.

It was now or never. Peering through the front and rear sights, she aimed at the alligator and squeezed the trigger.

It had only taken one shot to kill alligator. Holly briefly thought about a second shot, but she couldn't be sure what she was shooting at because both the alligator and Dillon were still tangled up.

The alligator relinquished its hold on Dillon.

Marching forward, she waded into the water, keeping the AK on target.

The water had become calm again, and Dillon had floated to the surface. She expected the alligator to launch a surprise attack, but it never did.

Now in waist deep water, Holly looped the AK over her shoulder and rolled Dillon over on his back. His eyes were open a slit, and she looked for movement on his chest.

"Don't die on me, Dillon!" she yelled. She slapped his face. "Don't die on me!"

There was no response. Putting her index and middle finger on his jugular vein, she noticed a faint pulse. "You're not dead yet! You hear me, Dillon Stockdale? Fight! You have to fight!"

Holly dragged Dillon through the water, the air cool rushing over his face and he reactively gulped a lungful of air, sputtering water out of his mouth. He coughed.

Dillon opened his eyes to a foggy and unfocused landscape of swaying trees and murky water sloshing around him. He blinked once, trying to force his eyes to focus.

He was on his back staring at the gray sky. A shiver captured his body.

A sensation came to him that something or somebody was dragging him through the shallow water.

The alligator!

His hands slapped the water in a feeble attempt as he struggled against the hold on him. With all his strength, he clawed at whatever had him. It was like his mind was disconnected from his body and he had no control over his movement.

He was being dragged through the water, but the sensation was different now.

Somewhere in the distance a dog barked, and a woman said something. Maybe it was a hallucination. His mind felt drugged, and he fought to stay conscious. The world started to bend, the trees moved and came alive, green fingers reaching to him. Dillon put his hand to his face trying to protect his eyes. He squeezed shut his eyes and opened them to the clouds coalescing into grotesque shapes.

"Stop fighting me!" Holly yelled. "Keep breathing!" Coming to the shore, Holly heaved him on dry land.

He became acutely aware of the cold breeze washing over him and he shivered uncontrollably until finally he passed out.

He woke later, vaguely aware of something warm and rough licking his face. Dillon closed his eyes and turned away. With a weary hand, he tried to shoo away whatever it was until an overwhelming fatigue came over him. His hand fell to the side, and he gave in to the need to sleep.

For hours he shivered and drifted in and out of consciousness. He watched the sky turn blue then dark; listened to the sounds of the night crickets and the trees rustling.

Smoke filled the air, and Dillon was somewhat aware of a fire, crackling and sizzling.

When he tried to move, his body felt like it was a lead weight. A fuzzy image of a person stoked the fire, sending embers into the air. A dog whined, an owl hooted, and Dillon drifted off to a fitful sleep.

Time meant nothing anymore. Seconds or minutes passed, or maybe it was an hour or a day. He couldn't be sure in his drugged state of mind. He was vaguely aware of being on his back, strapped into a stretcher of sorts. He tried to speak but his mouth wouldn't work. Hour after hour, he was jostled as he listened to the rhythm of hooves upon the earth.

Clouds floated by, misty rain fell upon his face.

Then the hard stretcher didn't feel so hard anymore. Hands flew over his body, turning him, lifting him onto something soft. A man spoke something to Dillon and he tried to answer, but the effort was too great. Keeping his eyes open and his mind focused required a herculean effort that escaped him.

Bed springs creaked and he felt the weight of something warm next to him.

He drifted back to sleep. Voices came and went, a door shut, various cooking smells wafted in the air.

When he woke, he became conscious of something warm and rough licking his face. He moved his hand and much to Dillon's surprise, it worked.

Reaching out, he let his hand drop to a large shape, something warm with rough fur. It moved and he immediately recognized the shape belonging to a dog.

"Buster?" Dillon's voice was weak and gravelly. "That you?"

"Yes." The woman's voice had a tinge of relief in it. "That is Buster." She moved closer to Dillon until her face was near his. "Tell me my name."

Dillon looked at her. "What?"

"What's my name?"

"Holly." Dillon looked around the room. A kerosene lantern illuminated the room with bare walls. There were two open windows on opposite sides of the room. A breeze came in, fluttering the curtains.

"Where am I?" Dillon asked.

"Remember the fish shack we stopped at?"

"I'm not sure."

"Remember the old-timer who gave us dog food?"

"Sort of."

"We're at his shack."

"Huh? I don't understand." Dillon turned on his side and tried to get up. Dizziness assaulted him and he put his head back on the pillow.

"What's the last thing you remember?"

Dillon didn't immediately answer. He let his mind work, trying to recall his last memory. "The fish trap. I remember checking the fish trap."

"Anything after that?"

He shook his head. "Not really."

It was quiet in the room. A cool breeze came through the window rustling the curtains, Buster scratched a flea, and Holly observed Dillon as his mind whirled, trying to remember.

"Oh wait," Dillon said. "I remember something now. An alligator. There was an alligator! Oh my God, my leg." Dillon's eyes darted from Holly to the bed. "Do I still have my leg?" His voice was frantic.

"Yes, your leg is okay. Badly bruised, but no broken bones."

Dillon let out a big breath. "Thank God."

"Can you wiggle your toes?"

"I can."

Holly explained to him that she saw the message he wrote in the dirt that he was checking the fish traps. She followed his tracks and when she heard Buster barking she knew something wasn't right. When she got to the lake, the alligator was already thrashing him in the water, trying to drown him. Looking for a weapon, she found the AK he had left propped up against a tree, so she fired a practice round before killing the alligator.

"I thought you didn't like guns."

"I don't. Never said I didn't know how to use them."

"Even the AK?"

"Yes."

"How?"

"I watched you."

Holly explained he must have had a dry drowning. "If any water had gotten into your lungs, you would have died by now from pneumonia or a lung infection." She told him she had made a stretcher using nylon cord and strong sticks, and that she had tied him in. "It wasn't the most comfortable ride, but we made it. It took me longer than I thought it would, but we made it back to Henri's place."

"Who's Henri?"

"Henri Delacroix. We're at his fish camp. Remember him? We stopped at his place and he gave us directions to where the plane might be."

"He was the one who gave us the fish trap."

"Right, and dog food," Holly said. "You hungry?"

"I could eat. What's on the menu?" Dillon asked.

"Alligator."

A knowing grin spread across Dillon's face. "In that case, I'm famished." Dillon put his head back on the pillow. "Give me about a day and I'll be ready to go again. I've got to find Cassie."

"I'm sorry, Dillon," Holly said. "That won't be

necessary."

"What are you talking about?"

"While you were unconscious, another survivor managed to find his way here. I found a picture of Cassie in your wallet and I showed it to him. He said he recognized her because he had helped her with the overhead bin." Holly dropped her gaze and looked away. "I uh, I uh..."

"What?" Dillon asked.

"I don't know how to tell you this."

"Tell me what?"

Holly cast a glance at Henri, who was standing in the doorway. He nodded for her to continue. "The man said he saw the seat she was in get sucked out of the plane."

"That can't be," Dillon said. He propped himself up on the pillow. "It can't be. No, I don't believe it. How did he know it was her?"

Holly came over to Dillon, sat on the edge of the bed, and put her hand on his. "He said he overheard her saying her real name was Calista, which is also his daughter's name. That's why he remembered her. It means beautiful one, doesn't it?"

Dillon said nothing, staring blankly at Holly in disbelief.

"He told me she had on a dark green Tulane t-shirt. I'm sorry, Dillon."

"I still don't understand. How did he make it here? Wasn't he injured? How did he survive?"

"I don't know. He said he remembered the plane disintegrating seconds before it crash landed. He was thrown out of the plane, away from the cabin. When he came to, he said he was laying in marsh grass. The only thing he wanted to do was to get out of there." Holly paused. "Dillon, it's time we go home. You saved my life, and now I'm saving yours. We will leave to go back to my ranch as soon as you're able to ride."

Dillon turned his head away and withdrew his hand. "Go. Leave me alone."

"I'm sorry, Dillon."

"Now!"

Reluctantly, Holly rose, left the room, and closed the door, leaving Dillon to his thoughts. He had failed his daughter, his wife was dead, and now there was no need for him to return to his home or to the life he knew. Lying in bed, he pounded the mattress in frustration, wishing the alligator had drowned him. It would have been so easy to die, and then he would have been reunited with Amy and Cassie. But that would have been too easy, too simple.

Living was hard, dying was easy, and Dillon wished he was dead.

Several days passed and when Dillon was ready to travel, he and Holly said good-bye to Henri. With a heavy heart, the weary travelers headed west, back to Holly's ranch, back to an uncertain future. Even though they hadn't been gone that long, Hemphill, the town of Holly's childhood, the place that had shaped her into the person she became, had been taken over by a deadly bunch led by a man known as the Boss, a man Holly and Dillon knew as Cole Cassel.

Epilogue

On a parallel journey, not far from where Dillon and Holly were, Cassie, Ryan, and James plodded on.

Days of struggle foraging for water and edible plants had cast a gloomy pall over their steadfast resolve to live.

During days of lonely walking, they had not seen or heard any human habitation. The late October sun was unseasonably hot, the air thick with mosquitoes, and sweat stained the clothes of the ragged bunch. The woodland and swamp stretched before them, the vastness of the Atchafalaya Basin daunting.

There was no hour of rest for footsteps heavy with fatigue, and when they could no longer travel, the weary travelers sat down and made a poor camp under an oak tree.

The night was unbearably long. The three tossed and turned on the hard ground until finally, they each fell into a fitful sleep.

During the night Cassie woke and gazed at the twinkling constellations, trying to remember the names from an astrology course she had taken as an undergrad. Focusing on the stars and the Milky Way, she forgot her dire predicament for a moment. She relished the brief reprieve until Ryan stirred, bringing her back to their unpleasant reality. Cassie turned on her side and propped an elbow on the ground.

"Are you awake?" she asked.

"Yes," Ryan whispered.

"Do you think I'll ever get back home? My dad must be going out of his mind by now."

"I'll get you back home, one way or another. I promised you I would."

"Ryan, how? We're out of food and we're down to one bottle of water between the three of us. We're lost and you know it."

"I'll get us out of here," Ryan said. "We have to keep traveling west. Cassie, don't give up. Ever. As long as you're breathing and as long as you can put one foot in front of the other, you can go forward."

"Houston might as well be a thousand miles from here. We'll never get there. I'll never see my dad again." Cassie's voice cracked. She turned her head and sniffled.

"We're not going to Houston," Ryan said.

"What? I don't understand. You said you'd take me there."

"I have something to tell you."

"I'm listening."

"My parents said that if I was ever in trouble that I should go to the city of Hemphill, the county seat of Sabine County, which is across the Sabine River. We aren't that far from there and we'll be able to find someone to help us."

"Really? Do you know someone there?" Cassie sat up, interested in what Ryan had to say.

"I know *of* someone."

"Who is it?"

"Nobody you know. But it will be someone we can count on. I'm sure of that."

"At least that gives me hope," Cassie said. She put her head back down on the ground. "It should be morning in a few hours so I'm going to try to get some sleep. You should too."

While Cassie slept, Ryan lay awake, letting his thoughts drift to the immediate problems he needed to solve. They were teetering on the edge of life and they needed shelter, water, and food. Unless he found those basic necessities, they'd all succumb to the elements.

Finally, Ryan drifted off to sleep.

The night crept by, the stars slowly giving way to a distant morning light, bringing a new day and different challenges to the survivors of an uncertain world.

END OF BOOK 1

About the Author

Chris Pike grew up in the woodlands of central Texas and along the Texas Gulf Coast, fishing, hunting, hiking, camping, and dodging hurricanes and tropical storms. Chris has learned that the power of Mother Nature is daunting, from floods to category five hurricanes, to slippery ice or desert conditions, all of which has been experienced. It pays to be prepared.

Currently living in Houston, Texas, Chris is married, has two grown daughters, one dog and unfortunately three overweight, worthless cats.

Chris is an avid supporter of the Second Amendment and limited government. Chris has held a Texas concealed carry permit since 1998, with the Glock being the current gun of choice.

Got a gun question or want to know Chris's thoughts about the first rule of a gunfight? Or maybe a favorite knife? Or the choice of a rifle for any environment? Then email Chris at Chris.Pike123@aol.com. Your email will be answered promptly and your address will never be shared with anyone.

Before You Go...

One last thing. Thank you, thank you, thank you for downloading this book! Without the support of readers like yourself, Indie publishing would not be possible.

The other way to show your support of an Indie author is to write an honest review on Amazon. It also helps other readers make a decision to download the book. A few words or one sentence is all it takes.

So please consider writing a review. I will be forever grateful.

Also, this book has been edited, proofed, and proofed again, but mistakes or typos are bound to happen. If you find a mistake, email Chris at <u>Chris.Pike123@aol.com</u> and it will be corrected.

Uncertain World
Book 2

Book 2, Uncertain World, is next in the series. The stories of Dillon, Holly, Cassie, and Ryan continue for an unforgettable story about life after the EMP, personal struggles, and ultimate redemption.

All the best,
Chris

Made in the USA
San Bernardino, CA
18 April 2017